I0746880

Other books by Sherrie DeMorrow:

The Knight and Daye series:

Knight and Daye
Cloud of Dreams
The Elder Rose
All The Land
The Little Bird
Beyond the Land
A Little Princess
Romancing the West
The Silver Millions
The Painted Chapel
A Hound's Desire
Space of Things

The Young Dr Huer series:

A Beginners Realm
Flight Into Space
My Brother, Draconian

MY BROTHER, DRACONIAN

BY

SHERRIE DEMORROW

Published 2021 by

Lightning Source (UK) Ltd
Chapter House,
Pitfield,
Kiln Farm,
Milton Keynes
MK11 3LW,
UK

Cover Art Design by Sam Wall

In Memory of Tim
With love

PREFACE and AUTHOR'S NOTE

Please be advised this novel is a continuation of a backstory of the character of Dr Elias Huer of the *Buck Rogers in the 25th Century* series, old and new, but I am basing it on the television series that aired from 1979-81. However, the events in this story PREDATE the television series, and cover Dr Huer's younger years, up until the series itself. Then the story ends.

I did write to gain permission from Universal to use this character, but I got no answer. Hence, I am writing these new series of books in loving tribute to the man who portrayed Dr Huer in the television version, Tim O'Connor. Tim has made appearances in several of my books, re-imagining a character for him in the *Knight and Daye* series that I just completed. This story does draw from those books, to put a cohesive backstory to the Dr Huer character. I want to give the man more than just a 'desk job'. I want to see what his early years were like, for example: what he thought, how he lived. Was the 25th century all that it was cracked up to be, as it was shown on television? Why did Dr Huer seem so sad? I want to see the good doctor in action, like Buck Rogers from the previous shows. A lot of the time, the doctor was so dead-pan serious, it made me wonder. An actor of the older generation would display vast amounts of seriousness to a role that was expected to be serious. However, the portrayal was so good, it made the character dull and boring. I do not believe (and I refuse to believe) that he was really like that. There is much to explore, and to examine the nature of Dr Huer is an excellent example of fandom, indeed.

Some place names and characters given are based on the television series (like New Chicago, or Anarchia, Kane and Twiki); acknow-ledgements for this had been made previously.

Other characters, mentioned or otherwise, are fictional and loosely based on people known of by the author, or from the previous *Knight and Daye* series.   Any personalities referred to herein are used (again), in loving tribute.

If there is anything amiss, please write to the publisher, and it shall be corrected.

CHAPTER I

I felt a sense of accomplishment: saving girls and exploring, one ship at a time. Space seemed like a dark, cold and lonely place, but with a wife and an onboard computer system, it was better than modern opinion. It was like I was insisting on rushing the sun out, as soon as possible, and getting in the good rays of life.

We were out in the starfield lightly searching about, when suddenly I heard that soft little peppery voice.

'I'm scared Elias,' Cindy quivered. 'Let someone else explore this quadrant. We've done enough. I want to go home.'

'Cindy,' I argued, 'We're in the middle of an important breakthrough here. Don't you want to know what's out here?'

'For tomorrow. Not today,' she answered quietly.

I hesitated, then told her, 'You don't know what you're missing, what we are missing. The Directorate would kill for this information that you are simply just passing by in the wind.'

Cindy stayed her ground. 'Let some other person find out what's out here.'

I relented, and turned the controls to return to Earth. 'Meg, we're going back.'

'Don't you want to explore this? It is quite a find,' Meg cried, 'I'm currently tabulating the data.'

'Just do it, please,' I ordered.

'You asked for it.' Meg was already regretting the loss, but kept whatever data she had attained on file for future use.

The console lights whirred a bit, then quieted down. The ship turned around and we were heading back home to New Chicago. We went through the stargate again, in all its tumbling glory. It wasn't really as special as the first time around, but going through it again proved it was a stable prospect for Earth's potential use. Probably a potential for someone else, too, but I would rather it be for us. Discovering such a portal to the unknown posted so many options and possibilities for those on Earth. *What could we do with such an object,* would be the obvious question of the day. Man has screwed up bad in his past; the Big Blast was the ultimate in human suffering. I soon reflected on that dream I had, about the Dagji referring to the event as a nuclation. I found the idea weird, coming out of a dream, but anything could happen these days.

I was saddened that Cindy was unable to continue the trip, a trip of a lifetime, mind you. She wasn't as bold as she used to be, as she was more on her own in Anarchia. It seemed that coming to me and our resulting marriage had softened an otherwise tough-shit-rogue exterior of hers. I truly missed this and lamented that one Cindihan died and one was reborn. She hadn't changed that much, but the fact that she came such a long way from there, only to be fattened-up, so to speak, by easier living, like we all were.

The flash of stars greeted us, with a thunderclap noise, making me feel like a new man. Yet, it was we who discovered and went through the stargate. It counted for something. I could not think of any other accolade than *that*. I felt we'd done enough anyway, and my sense of newness was fed into me by my experience. We passed through once more, and soon our own system appeared.

The familiar planets looked boring by this point; I really was itching to get back through the portal and do some serious exploring. Maybe with another pilot, while Cindy was looking after our children. I giggled at the notion. I wonder if the stars missed us, but at least we completed our mission. Meg had enough data to share with the Directorate; the incomplete stuff will be dealt with later, probably from someone else.

We passed the planets and moons, respectively, when I felt a thud sensation.

I panicked. 'What was that?'

'The ship is nearly out of power,' Meg answered, 'I am going to have to set down on one of these craterous rocks to recharge.'

'Great,' I huffed. 'If you must, I recommend you go to the moons of Saturn. There is one called Dracos in the far corner.'

Meg asked, not understanding the full reasoning. 'Any reason why Dracos?'

'I want to visit my brother. He lives there now,' I revealed.

'Ah, well, in that case, yes, sir,' Meg obeyed.

Dracos. The small moon my brother lived on since college. Draconians did not like to think of it as a moon. They thought it was a planet. Their own planet, with tied-dyed molten rock looming on the outskirts of the cities. They were refined citizens of their own species, even though they were still human, with their own culture, some language differences, but nothing incompatible with our own.

They could not miss their mark, as they were trying to make their mark on their world. But who knows what kind of mark they would make on the universe, if they had the opportunity to grasp it like I did, via this stargate? I didn't like the prospect, and decided to keep this bit to myself. If they wanted to go out exploring like Cindy and I, then let them, and let them have the glory of the stargate all to themselves. Just don't say it came from *me*.

We looked around to see where we could land so Meg could recharge the *Crab*. An incoming message had appeared and the landing crew on Dracos had spotted us. Meg went through the rigours of her messaging system, telling them of her 'issue', and the Draconians allowed our ship to land.

We stepped off the *Crab*, when we were greeted by my illustrious brother.

'Good to see you, Elias. What brings you to our humble society?'

I stopped dead in my tracks, unknowing about this uncertain reunion and found it a shock seeing my brother among the guardsmen of Draconian society. *Where those guards from a different squadron, or from an upwardly mobile being?*

The Saturn moon of Dracos looked immense among the spinning asteroids nearby. The rings were full of them, and from a distance, it was difficult to imagine such a wonder of uniformity. Everything was in the exact position and danced around as if it were at a party. I was amazed my brother had access to this. I would not have been surprised if he danced on these rings himself.

To protect themselves from these asteroids, the Draconians built a shield, as well as a laser to shoot down any stray ones that get too close to them. The atmosphere was breathable, at least, and the enriching environment was something to see.

It resembled New Chicago on various fronts: the new buildings, the sleek transport designs, the people coping and creating a fusion of societies from Earth that blended well. It seemed that Silage's contribution would be appreciated, as every person on Dracos seemed like they were a mix of everything and anything the old Earth could muster. A range of dark haired, flashy eyed, beautiful women meshed with the stars, making them more stunning; the men were likewise attractive, almost soldiers in their field. This reminded me of my first meeting with the Kane brothers long ago, when their mother was notably stunning, though she was an Earthbound through and through. It looked like they took this on board their society. I now saw why Silage was attracted to Dracos. It was a way toward personal growth. He partook into the indestructible realm of a society run by the Emperor Hansfor. At least *he* thought so. However, my bone of contention centred around his interest in Cindy.

I was hoping I'd move on from him, and concentrate my skills as a pilot, maybe even a scientist (as everyone expected). *But no.* I saw him, clear as day, as if he paled it from the first moon. *He had his shot with Cindy, what else was there?* Considering he and I had not gotten along too well over the years, maybe it was a way toward reconciliation. More than likely, it would be an unwelcome path to tread on. Being cordial with her was one thing, but the conscious flirting was another.

And he addressed me likewise. 'So, Brother Elias, what brings you to Dracos?'

'Our ship lost power and needed a recharge. We landed here, thinking of you actually.'

'How convenient,' Silage cooled his sly tongue. 'Still, it is a fond
pleasure to see you and your wife again.'

He went up to kiss Cindy's hand. 'Likewise,' she responded.

He added, 'We are now family, no?'

'You can say that,' I gave a slight stir in my voice.

'How's married life treating you?'

'Good,' I put my arm around Cindy. 'But just remember, this lady is
mine.'

'Whatever you say, dear Brother.'

The snide and cocky attitude he displayed hadn't surprised me.

From a tender age, we discovered we were not meant to be close, as
such; especially since Silage delved into those chapters of the Irish
book we discovered in our room, during those formative years growing up. He now seemed more daring, bolder, and had a glorious confidence that could paint the ancient highways of Earth.

Though he seemed more adversarial to me, he was still the charmer.
'While you are planning to remain here, on my world, would you like
to stay at my place?'

'That is kind of you,' I replied, hoping Meg didn't take too much longer to recharge.

It was sad we had to remain here, without communication with Earth. The problem with the ship was that the systems were all electrical, which was what needed charging. The boosters, thrusters, engine, and communication systems. God, it would take some time before everything was ready for our return to Earth. *If we only could get this over with!*

I had not spoken to Pemur since we'd left and by now, I wondered if he worried about us. I figured he'd think we were exploring, and there would be reams of data to consider. Maybe there could be a way to communicate anyway, at least to tell him we were alright and on Dracos for the time being. As Silage was family to me, it seemed a plausible solution.

Problem still was the stargate and the decision to keep it from my brother and his fellow Draconians. I was pained to have to do this, as I had no real orders not to, but I took it upon myself to make it an order for me. I did not wish to see our enlightenment become a master-race machine for the Draconians, using it to conquer, maybe. I was not up on Draconian culture, but I knew it was aggressive enough to pull something like this off. Looking around, the society alone convinced me. I hesitated to be an informant to them, even if all I wanted to do was to say 'hi' to my wayward twin.

CHAPTER II

One of Silage's guardsman allowed us transport that hovered above the ground in a silent path. We were taken on a small tour of the immediate city, Ahnkhor. Silage was very quick to point out some sites, such as where he went to school, where he hung out, and the like. I took it all in, and the place was no different from New Chicago. *No better, either.* I was just in a society of Earth's descendant-survivors, or next generations of them, living elsewhere and making it worthwhile. They made up for what was lost and it showed. Buildings had to be larger and sturdier. People had to live by discipline, taught from an early age. Life had to be better, bolder, larger. Oh, there were possibilities here. I can see why all this came to the attention of Silage.

'So you see, Elias,' he proudly stated, 'You can have a decent life here, just like on Earth.'

'I'm intrigued,' I muttered, unamused.

I was hoping we would find refreshment soon. My stomach was crying out and Cindy was getting into those unstable moments of hers. Silage saw this and took it kindly.

He soothed her. 'We'll be going to a lively place, where there is food and entertainment. How about it, sweetheart?'

'Sounds great,' came her answer.

A few miles away, he took us to an Indian-styled venue. The architecture around us emulated that which was on Earth.

It was a fascinating fusion of the old Middle Eastern, Asian, African and European styles that peppered Anhkhor's landscape.

Even the citizens had taken all the best bits and collaged them together in their clothing. Their mixed ethnicities gave them advantages that united them under one title, *Draconian*; all this made up for the hundreds of mixed up races which survived the Big Blast of old Earth. I found it grand to see how other cultures evolved from the disaster. They seemed to be doing quite nicely. All this beauty being wound up within a ball of strict societal discipline, was unsurpassed by anything I saw in New Chicago.

The best thing I could surmise from all this was Silage, and his interest in history and cultures. All the fusion around me reminded me of my growing up with his enchantments, fascination with books and emerging personality. I would be keen to see Silage in all this, with his contribution of our Irish heritage among everybody else's on Dracos. It would be safe to say he was correct in his pursuit of the 'old' of long ago. I wondered about that Irish history book which was possibly left at my place back home; I'd forgotten about it. Maybe Silage took it with him, it had been so long.

With all the busyness the city offered, Silage indicated a stop. The transport dropped us off, and we walked a block or two toward the place. It was just the three of us. His guardsman was left on the transport, as the occasion was more for family. He didn't think it was right to stick around, anyway, as Silage didn't need a nursemaid. It was amazing that the Draconians could *trust* him.

'We keep a close watch upon one another, but we know when to bow out when needed,' Silage explained to me.

'Ah,' I acknowledged, 'And how are the Kanes? I trust they are well.'

'Fine,' he smiled back. 'They both went for entry-level political positions, now closely working for the Emperor.'

I didn't know what to think; I was used to a more democratic practice back home. A one-ruler system kind of frightened me, as I recalled, and there were many in Earth's studded history. Whatever we were able to salvage, we found, and a myriad of mistakes were plain and clear as the devastation outside New Chicago. I already knew the revelation of our little exploratory journey that led to the stargate would be vastly compromised, just based on the style of government Dracos chose to live by.

'The Emperor,' I repeated in awe.

'Yes,' Silage explained, 'His family had ruled this moon, since the first landings here. They named it, and named their rulers accordingly. It seems boring, but uniform, nonetheless. After fifty or more years, you could hold an ocean here.'

'I see, and a whole lot more, ' I turned a corner with him, it seemed.

'It is really nice to see you both, Elias and Cindy.'

'Good to see you too,' I added, with a small amount of pride.

We entered the lounging restaurant with its bespoken architecture. It was a handsome site, yet reflective of what I recall from Earth. Yes, Dracos really does know how to entertain the masses, with additional stunning. Fine dining, with a floor show. A scantily-clad dancing girl entered the fold, with sword dancers surrounding her. The promise was there, but I didn't think it would prove deadly.

'I tried to get in on this too, early on,' Silage admitted to me.

I horsed around with him. 'As the girl or the swordsman?'
He beamed a glass fizzer at me. 'Very funny. Both, actually.'

'They'd allow a male dancer in this place?'

'Sure, it's okay,' he laughed, 'Everybody's welcome. Although the genders need to be opposite. If it were a male dancer, the swordsmen need to be female. Here, it is the other way round.'

'Of course,' I had a small drink given to our table.

'Wow,' Cindy mused, 'You're very versatile for a gentleman.'

'It's all in the game, my dear,' he took out a bunch of magically developed flowers from his pocket. 'My aim is your aim.'

'Um... I don't think so,' she accepted them anyway, but paused. 'I've been travelling with Elias. He's very efficient.'

'I bet he is,' Silage slithered his verbal way toward her. 'I am so certain that your days and nights with him are covered with scientifically mathematical globules of goo.'

I wanted to belt him one for egging on my wife again. I gave him a look, and thankfully he backed off. I can imagine him on that dance floor, wiling his petals, swinging to the music, making a show of himself. He became so conceited over the years, but still treated me with cordial respect, *just.*

The dancing still carried on, as our meals arrived and we ate. It was elaborate and delicious, as I never tasted such a heady mixture of spice, meat and vegetable. The drinks were pleasant too, but not as pleasant as what Cindy and I had once before.

Just before leaving on the *real* mission to discover that stargate, I remembered the fuquwer. I was certain not to inform Silage of our findings. This place, this culture, this *conquest*. I refused to mention anything of our doings or goings-on in space. Personally, I figured that Pemur would agree with my decision, as he did not know of anyone we could tell in the first place! I decided to keep quiet about the matter, and tell him a small yarn that wouldn't get us into trouble with the Directorate or the Draconians.

'Well, I just had a birthday, not too long ago, and,' I began.

'Oh, Brother Elias, so did I,' he shook my hand. 'And it was a sure treat for me, too.'

'I bet it was,' I slurred at him.

'So what did you do?'

'What did you do?'

'I asked first,' he said.

I blushed, 'You think there was more to it, don't you? Well, Cindy and I went exploring for the Directorate. It was just an average mission, nothing more.'

Silage couldn't believe his ears. 'Excuse me?'

'We just went out exploring, like Elias said,' Cindy continued on. 'When the ship needed to recharge, we landed here and decided to come to visit you.'

'Oh, how touching,' Silage drooled neatly, wiping his mouth.

I quickly asked, hoping he'd drop the subject. 'What did you do then, brother?'

'Biding my time, checking out the women,' he replied, 'And I am helping out with the Emperor's needs.'

My blue eyes widened, and the fascination came back. 'The Emperor, again?'

'You seem to have a fascination with titles, my dear brother,' he laughed, 'But I am assisting with his needs.'

I was sceptical. 'What needs?'

'My knowledge and information about things.'

Figures all that history would come in useful.

'Okay, so all your prowess had paid off somewhat,' I said.

'It had,' he got up, 'Shall we dance? There is a ballroom at the rear of the property, reserved for such delights.'

'I guess you don't bring your family here for nothing,' Cindy tittered.

'You're quite correct, madam.' Silage led us to a room where music played, similar to what we saw doing in that floor show earlier. It was slower, though, and showed more meaning. I resumed my partnership with Cindy, while Silage searched for a partner of his own.

Among the wallflowers, he gazed at them; they being most patient, waiting for the right moment in time for someone to dance with. He found an eager delight in a stout beauty, giving her a chance like the rest of them. She couldn't resist his wily sensors and the word 'no' meant nothing to him. It was an easy beat, good floor music. It reminded me of my good time past days with Cindy.

'This is lovely, Elias,' she said, 'I wouldn't mind living here.'

'I would,' I curtly answered, 'This place is not for me.'

'Well, I like this place. You're a dour lot of a scientist, you are.'

'Wait a minute,' I protested, 'I piloted the ship with you. I am more than a *mere* scientist!'

She kissed me and said, 'You are a scientist-pilot and the dumb-fuck days are way into the future. Let's live in this day, thank you.'

So she envisions me as my Dad? I cringed to think on it. I stayed silent and dared to no longer argue. It wasn't worth it, and it definitely would look tempting to Silage, who was pressing me for weakness. *Probably to get at my wife*, I wasn't sure, but to display heat now would be a bad idea. Public displays of affection, or intolerance would be indescribable here.

With the food, drink, music and good feeling all around, I would hate to be a killjoy, even if I did want to break it up. Nah, it wasn't like me to do such a thing, but if Silage got unto my wife again, ooh, let the madness begin.

CHAPTER III

The song ended, as another one began. Everyone changes partners at the song change, so Silage went a-wandering; the prowl for a new partner. I guessed I had to, too, and told Cindy to be careful. Again, my feelings were aroused, and not in a comforting manner.

'I will, Elias. I love you,' she told me.

I went to pick a cover-model wallflower, and Silage brazenly took my place with Cindy.

'Hiya, doll,' he cooed at her.

'Hi,' she answered, embracing him in a slow dance.

I hesitated in the dance a bit, just watching the two of them. I didn't think he would intentionally take her from me. Yet, I had to let it go, *it was only a dance!* I paired up with a gorgeous Draconian woman. It turned out she was a cover-model of one of the more popular magazines in Draconian society, *Dazzling Dracos.* Her dark locks, long legs and shiny, shimmering dress blurred my sight from Cindy. I had to forget my wife temporarily, hoping she was in 'good' hands. *No, that was Pemur.* This was now Silage who took the dance over. *Ugh.* He had Cindy for a distant while.

Then, the music took a swinging, intentional turn. Silage began to dance his way toward the doorway, reason unknown. I found it rude to leave my partner, but she thanked me, but found my distraction unwarranted. Her new partner led her to a more rhythmic two-step. I thought nothing of the moment, but when the moment's gone, it was gone. I soon raced to get Cindy back, and found it more and more disconcerting to think she would be with him; it was over in a second.

I had to give the girl credit. She was standing alone before me.

'Elias, what's the matter,' she cried in surprise.

I wanted to get Silage, but refused to make a scene, as Cindy was okay.

'Come on, we're going,' I ordered.

'Okay, okay,' she relented, looking past the figures, trying to catch Silage's eye.

We left him, and wanted to get back to Meg to see if the batteries were ready for lift-off. However, Silage soon appeared in the doorway, and offered to put us up for the night.

'It would be very difficult to get to your ship in this time of night,' he said, 'I have plenty of room, and I promise not to interfere.'

I held back, yet again, exhaling, before I agreed. 'Alright.'

Doesn't Draconian society beg for man and wife to co-exist together as one, even if there were multitudes of them?

He went on, 'I have clothing you could wear, as you might be here awhile.'

I was aghast. 'Awhile?'

'How long does it take for your ship to recharge?'

'I don't know. I've never done this before. I guess it's a few hours or so. I doubt it would take days,' I explained.

'Well, spend the time with me.' he invited kindly to us. 'I can show you things you'd never seen before. You did come here for a visit, re-member.'

I bickered at him. 'Don't you serve the Emperor?'

'I do, but it is part time. I can go higher, if needed.'

'So, you plan to remain on Dracos indefinitely?'

'Looks it,' he answered.

I sighed, looking at Cindy, who stood there, looking around the area in wonder.

'These sights are interesting and very romantic. Aren't they Elias?'

'They sure are,' I went up to join her. 'Thank you for calling me, and not him.'

The moon looked stunning at night, with a neon and phosphorus glow about it. I resumed my look at the stars. Looking for some-thing out there that could 'rescue' us. *Well, it wasn't like that*, but the discomfort levels around here were getting into higher ranges. Silage arranged for transport back to his place, where we bedded down for the night. I just wished Silage would bed down *elsewhere*.

******

And so, such was our first night on Dracos with Silage. True, he did show some form of compassion toward us; in fact, he was really outgoing. I assumed he'd do so for others as well, considering his manners and all. His decision to remain here, trying to polish himself as his own man, was not a bad one. I still thought he was a bit rough around the edges. What scared me was his sudden droning away at night; was it an old spell he picked up years ago, now implementing it in daily life? I woke up, hearing words paired off like fisting-cuffs, desperate to become the winner. He didn't let up and carried on his chanting for tad longer.

His appearance changed somewhat, too, from what I remembered at my wedding. I remember the clothes were a little bit sporty, bordering on the sexy. He had a more mature look about him, even though we were still in our twenties. The thick, luscious, chestnut-coloured hair sported light touches of grey. Well, I could imagine a spell to make you look younger, but why would you want to look *older*? That, I found very odd.

I moved around somewhat and found Cindy still sleeping. I didn't wake her, and I left the bed to go to relieve myself.

It didn't take long before Silage heard my bumps and growls in the night. 'Is that you, Brother Elias?'

I paused, but answered him. 'Yes, just going to the privy.'

There. I gave my lame excuse and headed back to bed. I was trying to satisfy my curiosity about him too. It had been a long time since we've bunked up like this, and much had happened since.

'Pity I did not hear the toilet burst,' he smiled at me.

I scowled back, 'What are you doing up at this hour?'

'Personal reasons, brother, personal.'

I got up close to him. 'How personal?'

He exhaled, and explained, 'It is just my early morning daily exercise. Some people walk, some people run, some people lift weights. I just happen to chant.'

'You are keeping up the neighbours,' I ranted.

'Ah, but in these festive dorms of ours, dear Elias, the walls have been soundproofed. I disturb no one.'

'Yeah, except us,' I snorted at him.

'Well, you are always free to go, out into the darkness, waiting for your poverty-class starship to take you back to New Chicago. What would they think of your scientific findings then?'

I looked at Silage with dismay. *Poverty-class, sheesh, what would he think of next?*

'You have an excellent opportunity to do research here, you know,' Silage continued on, 'You can study us.'

The thought crossed my mind, before it got flattened by an oncoming train of another thought of getting out of here.

'Studying other people's cultures was not what I had in mind,' I said.

'It is too bad, Elias, too bad.' Silage sighed loudly, waking up my little Cindy.

'Elias,' she called out.

'Over here, my love,' I answered. 'Just checking up on Silage.'

She got up and joined me. She gave both of us a hug.

'Wow, there are two of you,' she beamed aloud, 'I get to have more Huer.'

I wished for the best here, and decided to put my foot down instantly. The thought of Silage joining in sickened me to death.

'Get off to bed with you. I'll join you in a moment.'

'Awh,' Silage complained, 'I think it would be fun, just the three of us.'

I glared at him. 'Doing what?'

He swallowed hard and excused himself. With all my good intentions, I took Cindy by the hand and put her back into bed.

She whispered to me, 'Can't I stay up just a little while? The stars are in their right chambers tonight.'

I now glared at her. 'They may be in their right chambers, but you ain't. Now go.'

She begged, 'Please? It looks so interesting.'

I caved in, nearly like an avalanche, and allowed Cindy to stay. I put her in my lap and let her watch the stars. Too bad she didn't have paper on hand to tabulate anything scientific, just to make it *look* like we were busy. Who knows what more she would find in her doodling? I instead gave her hugs and kisses, to make it more plausible, when Silage walked in.

'Catching up on refreshment, I see,' he noted, looking out the window, 'The stars are made for lovers like you.'

I sneered, 'And you would know this?'

'Sure,' he replied, 'I've been with women. Good women too, some of them, I plan to marry.'

Silage, marry? Now this I had to see for myself.

'I'll bet,' I doubted his word.

I headed toward the window, where the light was dancing out of its own eyes. The stars were glowing and shining, creating an array of sparkle about them. Cindy gazed upon them like an eager child, and held me tightly. Not to forget about Silage, she included him in another family 'hug' which I'd rather forget.

'I never had a brother before,' she stated.

'Oh no?' Silage lent toward her, though not menacingly. 'You will find it a wonder to enjoy a sibling, even if one is an in-law.'

She tittered and laughed about it. 'But we're all family now, aren't we?'

'You're damn right,' I said, despite the rivalry with Silage.

'Whatever is mine is yours,' he offered her.

Wow, she mouthed silently, as the view got more playful. Each focal point of a star was faster now, and the positions had changed in the past few minutes.

'There must be millions out there,' she cooed in awe.

'Actually billions, my dear,' Silage spoke, 'But who's counting? Just enjoy them for what they are.'

I found myself envious of my twin, as he flippantly stated the facts, like the know-it-all that was supposed to have been *me*. It was funny in what he'd become. A sort-of-scientist, with his head always in the clouds. I was deemed to be the brains in the family, and now I found that my brains were being challenged. I just figured Silage was being Silage. He was good at some things, and I was good in others. Apparently, it wasn't something you tamper with on a cold winter day.

CHAPTER IV

Back on Earth, Pemur walked around the New Chicago Directorate Office. It was a cold day, but the temperature dynamics were at a comfortable 25 degrees Fahrenheit. The heat kicked on, and the computers were hot and ablaze with activity. A sterile office, it had its peculiar charm about it. Even the walls were somewhat coloured in cold mysticism, soft lights texturing their glow.

Still, it didn't deter Pemur from stating the obvious when he cried aloud, 'Where the buck are they?'

He nearly sobbed heavily when an assistant, Lt Selina Cayley, ran in to see what the fuss was all about.

'Sir,' she cried, 'What happened?'

'What happened?' Pemur got hot under the collar, and through honest tears yelled at her, 'What happened? I'll tell you what happened. The Huers are not back yet.'

'Space travel takes forever,' she dismissed his concern.

'It had been a few days already,' he sang to her in desperation.

'So, send a message to the ship. The ship sent one to us just before they entered that stargate.' The officer showed concern. 'Are you okay, sir?'

Pemur rubbed his face, trying to excuse his rashness. 'Okay. Yes, Lt Cayley, I'm alright.'

'I don't believe you, Oppenmach, 'You never bucked around and let loose like this since your wife died.'

'You didn't know me then,' he replied.

She got him up and put him on a bench, massaging his shoulders. The office, which had the sterile-coloured look of native glow, was in tatters, with papers and strongboxes haphazardly scattered in all the recesses of the room. So much for 25th century neatness!

She offered, 'Can I get you anything?'

'Yeah, you can,' Pemur answered, 'A case of good gin and some answers.'

Lt Cayley reflected on the mission we had and why we were not back yet. 'I am sure Cadet Huer and his wife are okay. They couldn't have far to go, without them showing up on your scanners.'

'Or maybe the *Crab* is faulty.'

'Possibly.'

The two looked at one another. Lt Cayley got up and went to get Pemur that cocktail he wanted, even though sounded in jest. She brought it back to him. He ripped the top and drank like there was no tomorrow. *Maybe there wasn't.*

'Want one,' he offered.

'Under the circumstances, yes.'

'Well, go to the fridge, and pick one out for yourself.'

She did, and went to give herself a tall cool one.

'Oh, a fuquwer,' she gasped.

'Only the best for my stable,' Pemur smiled.

She took the liquid and poured it into a glass. 'A toast for Cadet Huer. I hope he finds enough space for himself.'

'Hear, hear,' Pemur drank up.

'They couldn't have gotten this long without showing up on our scanners,' she suggested.

'Scanners or not, they're gone. Just where?'

They enjoyed the rest of their drink when a message from Lt Busdon lit up the monitor.

'Just checking to see how the Huer flight went,' he said with concern.

Pemur got up and viewed the monitor. 'Don't worry yourself about it. I am sure they are fine exploring the region beyond the stargate.'

'I guess that was a mighty fine surprise you gave them,' Busdon uttered.

'Not as good as the one which involves a talking computer,' chimed in Lt Cayley.

Pemur smirked at that one. 'Yeah, we'd given them an on-board Theopolis. The calculations Cindihan gave us should match the reality in what they are about to discover, or have done so by now.'

'It's been some time since Meg's last communication,' Busdon said. 'Maybe they're on their way back.'

'Or finding a vacation spot somewhere, you know those two.' Pemur replied.

He turned to another terminal, and tapped away, looking up details of the voyage and even the good ol' Huer name. The response given had revealed Silas on the Saturn moon of Dracos. Pemur hummed to himself, trying to do a mathematical calculation in his head concerning 2+2. He had a strange feeling that his favourite pilot, Cadet Elias Huer, had gone over to visit his twin on Dracos.

Meanwhile, Busdon signed off and Pemur was alone with Lt Cayley once more. She was also aware of the twin being on Dracos, and postulated. 'Maybe Elias went over to see his brother.'

'Possible, but not on a mission such as this. There has to be a reason for this delay,' Pemur continued huffing impatiently.

He attempted to send a message out to Meg, asking what was going on. A few tense minutes later, he got his answer:

Landed on Dracos; recharging batteries; Huer and wife went off to visit twin brother.

Pemur was semi-furious, and called out, 'That silly Elias!'

'Told you,' Cayley smiled.

'Well, there is a legitimate reason, but it wasn't entirely familial. Battery recharge.'

'Guess they don't make ship-chips like they used to,' she giggled.

He then ordered, 'Lt, assemble a rescue party. No telling what's doing on Dracos and I do not want Meg to be part of another world, or
any world except ours!'

'Sir, I am sure the Cadet is fine, and his brother is taking care of
them.'

'That's what I'm afraid of.'

* * * * *

'I can see part of Saturn's ring pattern from here,' Cindy eagerly
yelled out.

'Yes,' Silage pointed out, examining the findings with a mini-tele-
scopic device he had.

She went up to him. 'Can I see?'

'Of course.' He showed her how to use the device and soon, she was
seeing things out of her structure. it was like an old viewing gim-
mick from the late 20th century, with 25th century sophistication in
mind.

'Elias,' Cindy rang out, 'Look at this.'

She handed me the device Silage showed her, and wow, did I see
things! It was a different world from where we stood, and Earth was
a very far away planet now.

The Draconians probably had many a name for this set of stars, naturally, as they likely charted them years ago for navigation purposes like we did once. I got to see the asteroid ring of Saturn, plus a cool array of stars in their respective clusters. It was definitely a change from an Earth-bound point of view. I was certain scientists of New Chicago would be pissing to be in my heels right about now, at this new-found display. Pemur, especially. Yet, I was not here to work. I was here to enjoy myself, trying to develop a closer bond with Cindy, while taming Silage at the same time.

The stars gave their show for the moment, then dispersed like clouds. Others simply disappeared into the morning skies of Dracos.

'Pretty cool, Elias?' Silage walked up to me. 'I bet you that Directorate of yours would be itching to come here now to seek these findings.'

Frigid invitations didn't haunt me. 'I am certain they would love to explore your moon and your astronomical phenomena.'

Silage bellowed a laugh, 'My moon? Hey, I just live here, you know.'

'You could be living in New Chicago like me,' I snapped back.

Cindy stopped us before our rants became crossed-swords. 'Thank you Silas. That was something everyone can enjoy. If you keep tabulating them, they won't be as beautiful and you'd miss the moment.'

'Well put,' Silage patted her on the head. 'Well put.' He cupped her face. 'Thank you for calling me by my given name.'

She smiled at him; I was raining under the collar over her. A moment like this occurs but once a lifetime, twice if you're lucky. I thought it best to leave Silage to his own. I was sure Cindy wouldn't break rank from me. She seemed crazy about me since our times in Anarchia and Arachnia. *Nah, she couldn't.*

CHAPTER V

Silage later took me into a room of many chambers of Bathurst Lounge, where there were a host of women. Young, and all under thirty, they seemed cheap compared to Cindy. What scared me was I was correct in my knowledge of Draconian polygamous culture. Many wives were ideal, as breeding well was so important. There were no differences in society when it came to quality. Every person stood a chance to gain, whether a day-to-day job that helps run the society smoothly, a seat in Draconian bureaucracy (including the government), or just a Draconian guardsmen taking care of the Emperor, or whatever family he had. This was the highest point everyone lusted after, after the initial lusting was through.

'Although there are many more, I get to choose a wife. Maybe twenty, if I wish,' he said.

'Twenty wives,' I gasped, 'That's insane!'

Silage laughed at me, when a monitor beeped loudly on the speaker. It wasn't long after Silage arrived at his beauty den did he get a call from his friend Silver Kane. He put aside his dallying playboy exterior and moved into a more serious environment. His tone was just as serious.

Kane appeared on the monitor. 'The Emperor wishes to see you, Silas. He is most concerned about your troublesome brother.'

'Troublesome? Nah,' Silage dismissed, 'Elias has been very good. He's been with me all this time, along with his wife.'

'His wife is here? What the buck is she doing here? And what's more, what is HE doing here?'

'Pay it no mind,' Silage assured. 'They're just visiting me.'

Silver Kane got suspicious. 'Yeah, a visit to no-man's-land and beyond. No, there is something funny going on around here. Do you know why they came?'

'Their ship needed recharging, Elias said.'

'Well, it should have recharged and they should have left eons ago. I shall arrange an audience for you. You can explain it to His Highness yourself.'

'Sure thing, Kane.'

Kane switched off his monitor. He was not happy with the thought of Earthbounds like us on Dracos. True, the Draconians were once Earthbounds as well, but they outgrew those 'bounds' and evolved into the culture that sprung forth around us.

A young woman came up to Silage and cooed into his ear, nibbling at his shoulder. 'Want to join our bed party?'

'Not now, dear girl, not now. Maybe some other time, when I am not occupied,' he said to her.

'Too bad I'm not a meal for your affection, honey,' she answered. 'It would have been nice to see somebody's taste run down my valley.'

'Very funny,' Silage smirked, as he walked out to meet with his superiors. He left Cindy and myself to our own devices.

I looked around at the endless women. Some of them made eyes at me, some of them made faces at Cindy. Either way, it wasn't a place you wanted to stick around in. 'I do not wish to remain here. Let's go follow Silage, shall we?'

'Sure thing, Elias.' She kissed me boldly, right in front of all those females. *At last, the difficulty of Anarchia paid off!*

This did not go unnoticed, for as we left, I heard one of them say, 'There went a good opportunity.'

'Nice looking too,' another replied.

'And married, I see,' a third one noted our finger bands.

She must be one of the more intelligent ones.

We hastily followed Silage, and kept our distance, as he walked through the corridors of Bathurst Lounge. We saw him grab a vehicle that posed as a taxi. Hoping our covertness would go undetected, we grabbed the next vehicle and asked the driver to follow.

'It'll cost you some,' the driver said, 'I don't tailgate people for nothing.'

He gave me a big smile, as I fumbled through my change. Cindy had a better idea, and gave him a long standing kiss.

'Now for *that*, I will take you to the moon,' he said, and drove on.

I looked at Cindy, who pouted at my response.

'Elias, you struggled to find money. I gave the guy the only thing he would understand,' she said.

I huffed at her, but forgave the action. 'Next time, I'm buying, kid. No smooching on the job, y'hear?'

'Yes, sir,' she saluted.

The driver thought it was funny, as we heard him laugh it up. 'Where are we goin' to anyway?'

'Where ever that other vehicle is going,' I answered.

It was a good ride, and soon the other taxi stopped, as Silage exited the cab. I indicated to the driver to stop as well, so we could carry on our little self-contained, covert mission.

'That'll be five sahkrim, please,' he added.

I fumbled again, and Cindy did the honours. With another kiss, the driver accepted his fate and moved on.

So did we, after my elusive twin brother. When we caught up with him, Silage already entered the massive portals of Imperial Palace. It was good so far, until we entered inside. There, we came across a whopping amount of seers, doers, and hangers-on. The commencing crowds let us go forth incognito, until we had a run-in with a Draconian guardsman called Buckwolf.

'State your business here,' he said.

I gulped, and realising she couldn't pull the fast one on *this* guy, she simply fainted, due to the awesomeness of his body-building size. You never know if you might need those extra muscles. This fellow reminded me of the Kane brothers, but an all-in-one type. He stood over six feet, probably more, I figured. His face was beautiful, but savage looking. The clothing he wore was silver-lined, shiny chic, made from luxurious silk. His gun was ready to fire, and his eyes told us so.

'Be gone with your woman,' Buckwolf continued, 'Lest the Emperor finds something to do with you.'

I tried it on desperately. 'My brother was summoned here.'

'Oh, but were you? Now GO!'

We left the demanding fellow quite meekly, and joined the rest of the throng. We would rather spend our time elsewhere than with the person we encountered. I sorely wished upon every star in the sky that we were in New Chicago.

'If Twiki were here,' I passively hoped, 'He'd get us in. Or Theo at least.'

'They'll know it's us, or a possible threat,' Cindy reckoned.

'Maybe, if I can only get into the Palace,' I schemed.

'Forget it, Elias.' She dragged me away. 'You are a scientist-pilot, not a slip-one-over type of guy.'

'You're right,' I admitted, 'You're right. But you are not going to kiss him!'

'I never said I would, silly,' she snapped. 'And that guy? You must be kidding. No way! Yuck!'

Her revulsion toward Buckwolf was refreshing to me, but realising our defeat, I went back to the best idea we could muster at the time. 'I'm hungry.'

She asked, 'Know anywhere?'

'No, but we at least could have a look around,' I offered.

A restaurant, or any eatery, was a good idea, so we left Silage to his meeting and off into the Draconian night. Any place would do right now, and I did miss Twiki and Theo. But I knew Cindy was correct in the assumption that they would get us into some form of trouble, despite Theo's smart-talking ways. Having a drone around would look odd to the formerly Earthy, organically minded Draconians. They had no room for drones, ambuquads or anything of the like. I also figured that Twiki's personality and endless beading would get him shot-at in the most feral manner possible.

CHAPTER VI

Silage partook into the realm of the indestructible force that was the Emperor Hansfor. At least Hansfor liked to think that. Surrounded by guardsmen, not unlike the kind I saw earlier, He was led through and taken to the main chamber. A heady mix of Art Deco of the 1920s Western world merged with the Eastern concept of chic. The layout had many corridors, and the icing on the cake of one of them led to the Emperor.

The Emperor Hansfor was a tall guy, and slightly better fed than the others. He didn't want to show too much of that, so he did a regular exercise regime alongside his troops. They always kept in shape for those you-never-know moments. A dark, attractive gentleman, he had women squirming to meet him, nay, even marry him. It all comes from the sights, sounds and tears of the seers, the doers, and the hangers-on. Not much was posted for the latter, as they usually were scuffed away by guardsman and thrown unto the pavement of the night. The Emperor was surrounded by many; such was the case when you were a great man, leading your people. He was the founder of a minor Empire, which consisted of that small Saturn moon of Dracos. *Much more will be revealed*, he thought, *and conquered just as swiftly.*

He claimed all to be his own, especially his children. Prince Draco, the eldest, was pristine and brash, much like his father. Draco had ambition too, and wanted more out of the universe. A small moon never hurt anyone, but many more of them would gouge a city, bringing them to heel under their happy master. Happy, because he'd conquered it, and it was all his own. This shouted security, and the decor showed for it. Carved animal motifs in the wallpaper, and the throne itself displayed their fiercest charms among fruit, foliage and the attacking of prey.

The throne Hansfor sat upon stood on a dais; all thrones did, unless you wanted to be more ecumenical with your people and be among them. Problem was, Hansfor was the type who you bowed down to, not to integrate with among regular folk.

The dais was surrounded by a shallow pool of small creatures resembling crocodiles or alligators. Maybe both, as breeding could cross and new creatures emerge. There was no name for them as of yet, and Hansfor just called them 'pets'. He thrived on the extra protection. There were many attempts on Hansfor's life, all the way to when he was twenty-one when he took over from a previous, ancient incumbent. The animals also posed as mini-bodyguards, so he had an added bonus. *Let someone try to grab the throne for themselves.*

It took many stages of life to appease the climate to the now toughened natures. Decades of shaping the Saturn moon into an Eastern-styled paradise that took its people to the pinnacle of existence. They conformed Dracos into an entity to be reckoned with. Everyone helped to contribute to the societal meaning of 'chic or else'. They loved luxury. They loved hard work. They hated either to be compromised, but what they needed was *expansion*.

This Silas Huer, whom the Emperor wanted to see, was such a man he was after.   He did well in the Academy he was posted to, and served well in the little odd-jobs he was given afterwards. Now, he wanted to test Silas, and to see where his loyalty lay. He had a twin brother, Elias Huer, who (with his wife), was also on Dracos. Elias was someone to be dealt with at some point, the Emperor mused in his mind. But at least he had Silas, and Silas was going to tell him things he needed to know.

Silas kneeled toward the throne after entering the Emperor's domain. He couldn't understand why *he* was asked to come here. Was it something personal, like loyalty, or something more sinister, to the detriment of others, maybe his twin, maybe the Earth itself? He didn't know and at the moment, could not figure it out. The Emperor knew, of course. He wanted that twin brother on-the-loose and the information he *possibly* carried with him. He must have flown out here for a reason, and Hansfor wanted to know why.

'Silas Huer,' he barked loudly.

'Yes, sir,' Silas meekly responded.

'Your brother is here on Dracos, yes?'

'He is visiting me, naturally,' Silas insisted, trying to help me.

Hansfor pried further, 'Do you know why he is all the way out here? What is he, a scientist or something? A pilot? A dumb-fuck? What?'

Questions, questions; Silas had never been in this situation before. Not like this.

'I was told his ship needed to be recharged.'

'Okay, but why is he out here, far from Earth? On this moon? I thought he was supposed to be boring, or something.'

'To visit me,' Silas shouted, then lowered his temper. 'I could find out for you. I have ways. I have means.'

'Well, raising your voice to me isn't one of them, Silas,' the Emperor warned. 'I have several pets beneath me, and believe me, they ain't fluffy.'

Silas took a breath and pledged his cause to the Emperor. 'I will find out, or die, my liege.'

Hansfor noticed something rocky about him. 'You are too immersed in the history books, aren't you? I've heard of your keen interest. I don't care what you know or who you know it with, just get me what I want. Why is your brother here?'

The Emperor made a gesture to take Silas away from the throne to cast him out with the rest of the riff-raff awaiting his pleasure. That guardsman, Buckwolf, who harried us, now harried him.

'You better give the Emperor what he desires or...,' he indicated his head being cut off.

Silas winced at this and he had realised his loyalty. There was no going back. He loved me and my wife, as family, but otherwise the rivalry between us was present. And it got more complicated with a foreign leader involved. Silas was already embedded with Draconian culture, and mixed with Celtic mysticism, history, and lore, he was a very unique specimen on the lone Saturn moon of Dracos. Being at its school, serving society in his own meagre fashion, and now having to deliver information that could cause a great problem to the population of Earth. This will prove most interesting.

CHAPTER VII

Away from the clouds of despair, Cindy and I enjoyed Draconian culture like tourists. We saw its sequinned beauty, and sequential way of doing things. It proved to us to be an out-of-this-world experience, even though it happily was patterned after our old world. I still didn't know if Meg had recharged the ship, or even if its generators were still in working order. I thought it would be finished by now, or take another day or two to complete. I'd left my communicator back in Silage's place, so I couldn't contact her.

We found a place to eat, down by an old brick road, a popular hangout, so I saw from the crowd and full tables. As we sat down, I looked up from the table to see Silage wedging his intentions toward us. He looked most pragmatic, for a change, but dishevelled. It was site of uncertainty that he never allowed himself to reveal before. I guessed the opportunity was now presented to me and I relished it all the more.

'Silas,' I cried aloud, not giving up his personal nickname to the public. 'Over here.'

'Elias,' he answered eagerly, making his way to our table and sat down.

'You look haggard,' I noted, 'Where were you? Want a drink?'

'Yes, I could use one, thanks.'

A small piece of hesitation cropped up between us, when a waiter nipped by and put a pitcher of water on the table. He drunk it down in a flash, and whispered to me, 'I've been to see the Emperor.'

My eyes widened at their bluest. 'The Emperor?'

'Shh, yes,' Silage nodded, looking around him. 'Look, can we discuss this somewhere else? I fear the open ear.'

'Sure,' I agreed.

We slipped quietly out of our chairs, and into a more secluded den of foliage outside. Cindy checked around us to make certain we were alone.

'Why don't we go back to your place? It's probably more secure,' she suggested.

'And we could have a little something, maybe,' I added.

'Very well,' Silage came to his senses.

Hurried, we left the place and hopped aboard a tram which took us to his place quickly. We rode in silence. I wiped a tad of sweat on my shirt. A window was open above my head. The night breeze froze the salty air. Thankfully, no one cared. Everyone was doing it any-way. I couldn't imagine the flak I would get if I were in New Chicago. *I guess that was what made us different*, I supposed.

When we arrived back at Silage's and settled in, we had a long dis-cussion.

'Okay,' I demanded, 'What is up with you seeing the Emperor?'

'Oh Elias,' he slumped, grabbing a coffee, 'He knows you're here, and wants to know why?'

'We're here cos our ship's recharging,' Cindy admitted.

'He believes you're here for another reason,' he said.

'To pay you a visit,' I chimed in.

'No,' Silage disagreed, 'You've come out too far to be merely visiting.'

'You came to our wedding,' Cindy pointed out.

'Yes, yes I did,' he replied, 'But how did you get out here. Was it part of your honeymoon to visit Dracos? What were you two dilly-dally-ing in space for?'

I gulped as I took in the questions. I was still determined not to re-veal what we knew about the stargate and the possibilities it offered. I already guessed the possibilities it would offer the Draconians, IF I told them about it. I was unaware whether or not they knew about it in the first place. Weighing in all the details and spare parts in the mind, maybe being the boring-scientist-type would have been the better option after all.

I sighed, trying to do a cover-up on our mission. 'We were just dilly-dallying in space, exploring, screwing around. It wasn't serious.'

'I do not think the brainy, boring son of Elias Huer, Sr, would just go flying about in space, a no-man's-land, then come here to Dracos stating you were just up for a Sunday drive!'

He wasn't buying it. I wouldn't buy it, either, if there was a new uni-verse attached, a universe to capture as your own. Then again, I'd want to explore that universe first. No telling who you may be deal-ing with, if there were further life in those reaches of space.

'Elias,' Cindy quivered, hugging me.

'It's alright,' I assured her, then turning to Silage, 'Yes, we were exploring, but it wasn't what you'd think.'

'That is for me to find out, Brother Elias.'

Oh God, he's back on Brother Elias again. I wished I could smack him silly, for all those witticisms of his.

'This ain't the Dark Ages, you know,' I brashly spoke forth at him.

'It may be for you, my brother,' he threatened, 'If you don't tell me why you'd come out this far.'

I exhaled and shouted, 'Exploring!'

He shot back, 'Exploring what?'

I sat back, and begged Cindy to get a coffee for me.

She asked, 'With sugar or whisky?'

I stared back at her. 'Just go and do it.'

She turned to my brother. 'Silage?'

He allowed her to make it and we were now alone.

'One of these days, Elias, I'm going to get her,' he continued his threat.

I looked at him with contempt, and my fist was preparing for another go.

'I'm not that cruel,' he said, 'But this silence between us is most disturbing.'

Cindy came back with the drink, whisky, sugar and all, and I downed it like there was no tomorrow.

There probably never will be, at this rate.

'Elias,' Cindy screamed.

'I'm alright,' I stated, 'I knew what I was doing.'

Yeah, trying to one-up my stupid brother!

'I have direct orders from the Emperor himself to explain your whereabouts,' he cried.

Direct orders from the Emperor? Who did he think he was?

He knocked my hand with the cup still in it, before I realised what was going on.

'Why were you out here?'

I was shocked and disturbed by his action and decided to leave. I took Cindy out of the apartment and hastily ran toward the traffic outside, where we could get a ride away from here.

'We better look for our ship,' I told Cindy, 'If it's finished recharging, we're getting out of here, now.'

She agreed to it, and we went to find our ship. It turned out it was impounded by the Draconians, in order for them to see our flight path, IF they could get to the computer. I knew that Meg, in her ultimate wisdom and *none-of-your-business* practicality, would hide the vital information deep in a duplex storage system. She also had shut the ship down indefinitely, so if someone were to rifle with the controls, they'd be no response, or strictly manual usage. And there were no instructions on board. *It might as well be trashed*, so they say. Meg was clever to shut down. She was clever like that, and she also 'worked' for the Directorate. She might as well have been part of the Computer Council, but her dynodes were allocated to run *The Ancient Crab*.

Anything that dealt with issues relating to 'home' she classed as confidential, and rightly so. Thankfully, the Draconians didn't pry too much into her systems. It was just as well, as they weren't so hot on the complex technology she had in her, but it would only took a couple of clicks and pushes to find out there was a stargate in the midst. Thankfully, Draconians weren't *that* bright.

So, they took it and added it to their Squadrons instead; a sensible move, without the profit of knowing. It was now a pirate Marauder ship, and markings were put on the *Crab* telling it so. Tail-fins and tricolours were added to make it look like any other Draconian ship. It went a treat with the Emperor, who requested a ride upon it, seeing if it was worthy in his gang-busting flotilla of ships.

Meg meanwhile lay silent. She didn't give anything away and took the Emperor's interest in stride.

She felt his commandeering the vehicle was strange, as he wasn't the regular pilot who flew the ship. She felt the flow of engine oil around her guzzles and she still hadn't uttered a sound. Even the sound-on mechanism didn't work; she had shut that down, too. She was completely deaf unto everyone. Her clamming up allowed her room, sort of, yet, she knew she was being grossly violated by another party. Who came to that party was anyone's guess, but if the Emperor was involved, it must have been something. In checking her out, a mechanic supposed he would have put his own stamp on her systems. It did not matter, as she was the Emperor's property, for now.

CHAPTER VIII

Silage returned to his chanting, and plotted another way to salvage the information he needed. The chanting became stronger, and Silage was in the mood for it. It wasn't necessarily a mood, but it might as well have been one. It was intense, with some deathly definition about it. This did not deter him from the Emperor's pleasure, i.e., to find out what my purpose was on Dracos. Not that I had one, you understand. All I did was to go out and discover the stargate and return home. Nothing more. It wasn't my fault the *Crab* needed recharging. Silage, of course, thought my plan to be sinister, and would want to capitalise on it in a Draconian manner.

It didn't matter either way to Silage. He wanted glory and power with the Emperor. He wanted to look good, after all the years in the shadow of Dad and myself. Science obviously didn't swing with him, and his naturally good looks had shown that there was more to him that you met up with after school. His visions relied on little vials of liquid 'potions' he bought from online shops and mail order catalogues. Silage wanted to really recreate the olden times, possibly giving himself a cool balm or two of them. He looked at his small collection of books, including that Irish one that was in our bedroom during our formative years, which started this whole mess with him. He read through it and wanted to try his hand on making that potion that stayed age. Though he wasn't fifty yet (and neither was I, for that matter), he took interest in the story that went with the magic.

It was told that when Muffyhuer (then Conna of Cobhayr) and Cindihan got together, he took this potion to prevent himself from ageing. Cindihan was about forty years younger, and he didn't want to feel like an old man around her. Silage didn't feel an old man himself, but it would be nice to try the potion and see what happened at fifty. Silage was determined, though, to see what we were doing on Dracos.

Not to be swayed by human emotion, it didn't feel right for us to come all the way from Earth for just a mere joyride of exploration. Unnaturally, he turned back to his books and vials and things that went 'pop' in the daytime, as well as night. He figured if those spell-chants worked for the ancient Celts, they could probably work in this latter day era of the 25th century. Two thousand years was nothing to a few odd words and a glug of fluid that can turn your head around, if you weren't prepared for it. Silage didn't care about the risks. He knew them; he studied very well. He didn't want to displease the Emperor Hansfor; who knows, there may be something in it for Sil-age.

He found a spell which seemed tame, yet appropriate; a mind swap, which would make him me and me him. Not to overcomplicate things, it could make the moment awkward. Silage chanted away, re-ferring to the book to make sure he was doing it right. There was no liquid in this, just plain-chant and song. It would be really amusing to watch him, but equally dangerous. When he got to the highest note, he suddenly felt a flutter within him. He soon got flooded with memories of *mine* and he cried out, 'Cindihan!'

It became clear. The would-be dangerous twin brother of mine was now *me*.

'Cindihan,' he shouted again.

Cindihan? Wait, I thought she was forbidden to me... hey, wait a minute. Silage got up to look in the mirror. Nothing changed. It couldn't anyway, as he looked exactly like me, but for his dress sense. His face and body remained the same. Yet, he noticed that his newfound feelings of masculinity, and inner passions gave way to stoic, hard-core logic.

The mind swap scarily worked, and in his mind, he heard the child-like reverberations of Cindihan, calling out, 'Elias, Elias.'

Was I Elias now? He thought deeper; *oh yeah, being boring in New Chicago with that stupid noisy silver drone thing; that's Brother Elias alright.* The experiences flooded in: my meeting Cindihan in Anarchia, Eri-Cast in Arachnia, the long walk through the lonely deserted plains and the flight back to New Chicago with Lt Busdon. More memories came through: the wish to fly, the marriage, the drone Twiki with some new wattage hanging about his silver space, and Pemur Oppenmach, the leader of the Science Directorate who took on Elias Sr's work. *Ummm, these memories could prove useful to me.*

Silage rested, with not much to go on. Still determined, he tried to wrack through *my* brain to get the information. Soon, the flying lessons returned and then the simulations. The long sleep, where we met Zenix and her tribe. The times Cindy and I had in the bedroom; this Silage got very keen on. He seemed very interested in my wife and wanted her badly. Silage rose up from the endless reveries he attained and forced the pressure of memory to fully return.

Wait, wait... the final simulation where Cindy got clever with her calculations. *Calculations to what?* Silage continued his inner quest for the truth, while raping *me* at the same time. The squiggles at the sidelines got closer, the brimming imagination of the wife, the silliness of trajectories, the condescending nature of Pemur that led to…a stargate.

A stargate? That seemed absurd. Why would you want to go through a stargate unless... Silage thought again.

He had the answer; unless you wanted to explore *another* universe, maybe even conquer it. The Emperor would be pleased at this finding. He would really like that. Silage's thoughts brimmed as he took in the possibilities. He racked his mind again, and noted Cindy's intelligence, even if it were based on more primitive instinct. *Hey, she's smart for a young girl.* His mindset dwelled on her, probably too much. Still, she was my wife, and Silage knew she wasn't to be attained that easily.

But if Silage was now Elias, who was Silage?

CHAPTER IX

A funny thing happened to me on the way to the ammunition store. I fell back, as some bitter wind flew right past me. Smack down on the deck, I was struck bad. I could not make it out, and the wife ran to me in anguish.

'Elias,' Cindy cried out.

'I'm alright, doll, I think.'

I got up rather suddenly, and asked myself a dumb question. *Who am I?* I never had this feeling before, and then my insides all gnarled up on me. It didn't go away; nothing a peptic bottle could cure. As we had no home here, and we left leaving Silage's apartment already, we went to a motel to dwell and figure things out on the cheap. Our ship was nowhere to be found. For the first time, I felt stuck and alone. It was more frightening because I was on another world, not in the distant worlds of Anarchia, Arachnia, hoping someone would fly by to rescue me. *No, I was totally alone here.*

'Darling,' Cindy called me again.

I looked at her, with different eyes, strangely enough. 'Come here, you.'

'Ooh,' she yelped, as I dug in to kiss her, nearly crossing into boundaries of love.

'Oh, you pretty...'

'Elias!'

I heard another name. 'Elias?'

'Duh, you're the one I married, remember,' she reminded me.

'I'm not sure.' I banged my head against reason, and found there was none. I felt insecure at myself, but loved being with the ol' girl.

'Ummm, maybe you need to relax,' she suggested.

Cindihan looked like a pretty bell that chimed without reason, and here I was fighting it. It wasn't like me to do so, but the overall feeling I was getting felt too foreign.

'I love you, Elias,' she said, 'And I don't care if we're stranded on this planet.'

'Moon, Cindy, moon,' I tried to talk myself into reason.

I still found none. Elias was the name I was given at birth, but my personality had changed. I wasn't sure, but it felt as if I was wearing Silage's shoes, and they were a decent fit. Being a twin, some of our apparel were swappable, even shoes. Maybe.

Maybe.

I reasoned it out, and through the darkness, I finally saw some light.

He'd put a spell on me!

Oh my God, now he will find out about... so he could report it back to...

Now it was my turn to cry out, 'UGH!'

'What's wrong?'

I blurted out a sentence that to me, made no sense at all. 'Cindy, I'm telling you for your own good, but I am Elias, not Silage.'

'Yes, I know, duh,' she dismissed in haste.

'No, you don't understand. Silage put a spell on me. He has invaded my mind to find out about where we've been, and he's now me, and I am him.'

'Sounds like an old film I watched a long time ago. If you are now your brother, then, you should be dead hot.'

'Cut that out,' I retorted, fighting viciously the spell's effect on me. 'It's not funny. We are in trouble. God knows where they'd put our ship and now this. Those communiques are now known by my brother.'

'So if you're him and he's you, wouldn't that put him at a disadvantage?'

I looked at her. 'Go on.'

'Well,' she considered intellectually, 'If you're him, and he's you, he'd be ineffectual. You are now the aggressive go-getter and Emperor-seeker. You could widdle your way through a meeting with this fame and fortune type and tell him some crap that would satisfy him. You don't have to tell him everything, as discretion should still be with you. I hope.'

I realised my folly would come in handy here. 'By heaven, you could be right, Cindy.'

So what if Silage knew about the stargate? He'd go up to the Emperor as *me* and tell the old fellow, who in turn would sense something odd about him. The stargate story would prove inferior, compared to Silage's personality changing into mine.

And the stargate may even remain a secret after all.

'We've got to get to Silage, and fast, before he starts talking to the wrong people,' I ordered.

Cindy was sceptical, 'What do we do?'

'First thing is to go back to his apartment and change. If I'm going to play Silage, I must do it right. I might as well look it too.'

'You look it anyway,' she commented.

'In these clothes? Not a chance,' I answered.

We left the motel and headed back to Silage's place. I was unsure how I can impersonate my weird brother, but surely, I've got to make it count.

* * * * * *

When we got there, I sensed a change in the air, as I was let in by Silage.

Snidely, he greeted me. 'Hello dear brother Elias, or are you Elias?'

My voice was snide toward him. 'How so?'

'I've been getting the most fateful thoughts. Odd feelings. Something about you and Cindy's cruise, which led to a...'

'That's just nonsense,' I swiftly cut him off, knowing what the next word would be. 'Cindy and I were just passing pleasant memories, on an exploratory honeymoon, weren't we, dear?'

'I think so,' she then whispered in my ear, 'What if he knows?'

I nodded, and turned to Silage. 'You've got my memories, you should know what the wife and I were up to.'

He smiled, to which slime would make a great plaster cast upon him, in order to memorialise the event. 'I do, and more. I know she drew something silly, which led you both to discover the...'

I taunted him, mostly because he planned to give away our secret. 'What, dammit, what?'

'A stargate,' he dryly grinned, having out with it.

'A stargate,' I rode him out on this, 'So what? Those were precious, childlike drawings Cindy created to pass the time with.'

Silage pressed on. 'But you *did* discover a stargate, didn't you?'

Cindy looked at me, trying to tell me something. I keenly dismissed her, and had it out with my brother.

'Yes, yes, I did discover a stargate,' I goaded him, 'What's it to you? There could be many of them around here.'

'But only one leads to a different universe,' he said.

I wanted to cry. I wanted to scream. Instead, I punched him out. He fell on the floor and crumpled himself into a submissive ball. *A submissive ball that I was.* I was him, so now, I had to act quickly, before he awoke and told the whole Draconian brigade about Cindy's minor 'doodles'.

In a convoluted manner, he tried to get up, but I fought him, and put him back to dozy-land.

'In here,' I gestured to Cindy, 'Open the door.'

We stuffed Silage into bed, putting him at a disadvantage. He was now me, and there was nothing good ol' *Elias* Huer could say that was fathomable. Silas Huer, on the hand, well, that was another matter. Thankfully, I still retained my own memories, including the stargate, contrived from Cindy's drawings. Probably that spell wasn't a total charmer after all. But, I knew I had to play the part, and with all my determination, I ransacked his wardrobe. *No more straight pants for me.* I went through his clothing to find many a fancy item, similar to what I saw him wear to my wedding. I wanted to live the studded life he embraced, for a change. At least if I looked like him, and maybe spoke like him, we could get out of this mess alive, and back in New Chicago.

CHAPTER X

The spell was working, despite my misgivings about it, as I suddenly felt further change come over me, and it wasn't just the clothing. I felt an odd confident sensation, something which I never had in the first place. Furnished with an open-chested, leatherette top, and trousers to match, I experimented with Silage's sexiness, and wanted to see if I could pull it off.

I tip-toed my way behind Cindy, and grabbed her.

'Oooh,' she turned to me, looking carefully at my 'new' threads. 'I wish you'd dress like this all the time.'

We kissed. She looked at me again, her eyes taking in a huge amount of information. She playfully fainted on the nearby sofa. I rushed to her rescue.

'Remember, I'm still Elias, your husband.'

She awoke out of her trance. 'I am fully aware of who you are. You've been outwitted by your brother.'

'Silage will never outwit me. I just got the addition of *his* memories and personality traits.'

Cindy paused some, as I kissed her again.

'And I like it,' she admitted, 'You'll have no trouble convincing people you're Silas.'

She used my brother's real name for show. Her discretion was note-worthy.

'No, I won't,' I added. 'We have much work to do.'

Meanwhile, Silage was still laying in bed, silent, and I dared not disturb him. If he really knew where the stargate was, you would be hard pressed not to imagine conquest of the universe by Draconian forces. *The other side of the universe.* I could not let that happen, to that side or our side of the universe! Yet, I had to figure out what they'd done to our ship, if they did anything. I also figured I'd have to report to this Emperor of theirs to apprise him of the situation. It could not look suspicious in anyway, or we'd have it. I know he wanted to know what we discovered, but I couldn't have Cindy with me. So, I assigned her a task; to find our ship.

'Okay, but where do I look?'

'Well,' I mused, 'You could try where we docked, or an impound yard, which would be most likely. It was a lone, abandoned ship. Anyone could have taken it.'

'Why?'

'DUH, could you imagine the Draconians leaving it alone?'

'Oh yeah,' she thought, puzzled, 'But what would they do with it?'

'I don't know,' I now got frustrated, with postulations about the ship, and if they discovered our computer-programmable friendly Meg.

I looked at my watch, which had a secret attachment to the ship. I took it off and gave it to her. I then took Silage's fancy watch and used that for myself.

'There is a communicator on this,' I explained, 'Try to contact the ship, but use caution. You don't want anyone to know. If you're lucky, Meg will perk up, if she's no longer dormant. She'd shut down all systems, to prevent any tampering on a stranger's part. You'll have to tread carefully, but I guess you're used to it.'

'Thanks,' she remarked. 'A kiss for luck?'

'Sure thing.'

I gave her a kiss, and boy, did I kiss her. The spell worked wonders on me, even giving me the will to...

I embraced her dearly, like I never had before.

'I lost my face for you,' she said.

'I'm enamoured over you.' I cooed back, then forced her exit. 'Now, get going before Silage wakes up.'

I touched her on the rear, as she left the room. The watch was then activated, with little light bits flicking at her. I was close behind. However, something occurred to me, and I turned around to look for that book of spells.   I didn't know why, but I thought it might come in handy. *Funny thing to say when you're a scientist.* Now, I was thinking like Silage!

I soon found it and chanted a short passage appropriate for the occasion.

'Cast yourself well; In dozy-land ye shall dwell; When rabbits speak, or where they fell, may your sleep drive you to...'

Cindy popped back into the room, quickly disrupted the train going my way. 'Surely, you're not hexing him? After all, he's your brother.'

I put the book down. 'Okay. There, Cindy. Feel better?'

'Not if you're going to use Silage's power to hurt him.'

'Why, are you a moralist?'

'No, because he's all you got.'

'I've got you,' I sniggered, kissing her to always remind her she's part of my family.

Yet, I had something else to add, if not a 'hex' spell. 'Farewell, Silage,' I sneered at him, 'Or should I now call you Elias?'

I laughed maniacally, as I left the room with Cindy.

'Oh, Elias,' she cried, slapping me on the forearm.

We walked outside the building, upon the main strip of road that led toward the grand Palace of the Emperor. The streets were a lit, with a beautiful Draconian skyline that meant business. It felt funny wearing Silage's clothing for a change. I would hate to see him in mine. I chuckled softly to myself, thinking of how dull-witted he'd be now. But, I had my own memories as Elias Huer. I was certain he'd still carry his own, too. The spell merely added his to mine, and vice versa.

The watch I was now wearing (as opposed to the one I gave Cindy), had gone off at an alarming rate.

'Elias,' Cindy noted.

'No, quiet up you. Remember, I'm Silas, or Silage to you and me.' I then packed her off on her way, 'Now go find our ship.'

'Okay boss,' she saluted formally at me and scampered toward the place where our ship was docked.

The alarm still beeped, and I took the call. 'Yeah?'

Silver Kane appeared on the tiny screen. It looked like a television from the old days, manufactured anew.

'Silas, the Emperor wants an update on your progress.'

'Yes, yes,' I struggled to find the right words to tell him. 'I'm working on it now. I've got my brother to sleep and I'll extract the information we need from him.'

'You do that,' Kane advised, 'Though I cannot imagine how.'

'I'll get it,' I assured him.

'You better. He is anxious to know.'

'I'm sure he is.'

I ended the call. I felt relieved I convinced Kane that I was Silage. Now, to convince the Emperor, with the studded info-pack he reques- ted. Well, I'll have to mull over that one on the way to his Palace.

Kane then turned to his officer, Dhakrah. 'Silas seems preoccupied with something.'

'With his skills focused in the ancient past,' Dhakrah stated, 'I'd be preoccupied too. I'm certain he will deliver.'

'He better, or he's dead. It will be the best thing if we knew what Elias and his wife did in their space runs.'

'Maybe they saw a meteor headed this way.'

Kane snapped, 'If he did, shouldn't *we* know about it?'

The officer cringed. 'I guess.

The submissive personality of Dhakrah compared to Kane got under Kane's skin. In fact, Kane was rather peeved with him, but tolerated him, because he was one of the finest of the lot. Seniority helped as well here, and this gave Dhakrah an advantage like no other. Despite the finery, he was dismissed from Kane's presence, and walked away from the console to go to the recreation room downstairs. A good match of physical endurance would obliterate his more sensitive nature.

CHAPTER XI

I, meanwhile, finally made it to Emperor Hansfor's grand Palace. It took awhile for me to get out here, but thankfully Dracos was rather forgiving in this nature. Everyone was late for something, but just in a more timely fashion. The opulence of this place was astonishing, and very tight-fisted. It felt controlled, with an air of gloom mixed with pleasure. I was led to the chambers and met by Prince Draco, who eyed me unusually.

'Hello Silas, it is good to see you again,' he greeted.

The name Silas (as applied to me) fit weird, but I had to pull it off.

'Greetings, Your Highness,' I answered in return.

'My father's most anxious to know what you found on your brother's recent journeys through space. It may mean possibilities for us.'

Who did this guy think he is? Possibilities for those on Earth, not Dracos.

'Or it can be a grisly end,' I commented. 'Look, what my brother and his wife found was just a bunch of common meteors. Just asteroids in space.'

My nervousness seeped out, as I desperately tried to calm down and continue talking.

'You can tell my father that.'

I was led to the Emperor himself, and continued to be inspired by the decor of the Palace. All the richness here, surrounding me in a dom- inating fashion really had me thinking.

On Earth, the rebuilding left it just at a minimum, like a blank canvas; a blank white screen, where you could mould the place into your own. Some buildings I'd seen over the years had some ornateness. We didn't want to be too flashy about it. Just practical.

Maybe I could pull this off, or have myself pulled off instead. Referring to myself in the third person took time to get used to. Yet, in front of the greatest person on the planet, I had to *be* Silage. Then again, I had to get used to remembering to use the name Silas, for a nickname will never do for an Emperor.

The Prince Draco introduced us. 'Father, Silas is here.'

'I know Silas Huer, my son. You go now. The animals are waiting to be fed.'

'Yes, Father.'

He meekly left the room, as did the few guardsmen who were present. We were now alone. Alone in a room, full of imagined crouching beasts about to strike at you. Floral decor swirled around , either making you dizzy or making you need to scratch an itch (as if you had poison ivy). No doubt the wallpaper had some toxicity about it. Even the lion's claws made you jump; they were three dimensional. There were decals of lettering I could not make out. Probably their language, I reckoned. It's like I'd never been here before, yet, apparently I had been, for the Emperor remembered me. *Oh God, I've got to make this good, without giving the game away.*

'Silas Huer, we meet again,' the Emperor bellowed, 'Drink?'

Needing to go with the gag, I accepted. 'Yes, I'd like one.'

'Good. You know, we have much in common. We are from old Earth, remaking ourselves in space.'

He gave me a cup, and I waxed down the liquor so fast, it made *his* head spin.

'I didn't think an Earth man such as yourself would physically accept a potent mix of heady spice.'

I smiled, 'You don't know me. And to make a point, I was an Earth man.'

'Yes, yes, I see. I lived on Earth, too, before coming here to colonise this moon. My parents took me on a trip I would never forget, and after a few years of hustle-bustle, you know how it is, here I am.'

'In all your splendid glory.'

Hansfor pressed me. 'You then call yourself Draconian?'

'I like to think of myself in that fashion, yes.'

The spell was still working, becoming more and more potent as I spoke. My nervousness thankfully gave way to more confidence, which I needed to deal with such a character as this. Maybe we can get out of this alive. I tried to emulate Silage's eloquence, without telling him anything. So I explained it to him in the best way possible. 'Elias and his wife went exploring for the Directorate. She saw an anomaly and drew markings of it, but they were the product of her own imagination, just to pass the time on the ship. She's young, you know how it is when one gets bored.'

'Oh, I know boring. I remember it well,' the Emperor understood, still questioning me. 'So this exploration was just mere amusement, resulting from an overactive imagination?'

I pondered, and lied a bit, 'Yes, but they did see a hole in space, as well, yet it turned out to be an old star that died out many years ago. They paid it no heed. They were in fact on their way back to Earth, when it was decided they should land here to recharge and visit me.'

'I see.' The Emperor paced about, digesting what information I was comfortable in giving to him. 'Thank you for informing me about this. There are chambers in the palace where you can enjoy yourself.'

I couldn't believe he 'bought' my story, yet he invited me to remain in the palace. 'Chambers, sir?'

'Yes, you can pick your wives from them. I thought to allow you to some, as you wish.'

'Thanks,' I added dryly. Luckily, I removed the wedding band, now located within my pocket, figuring he was still a bachelor. I, on the other hand, was not, and if I still wore it, being Silage would be a hard sell for me. Jewellery and adventures don't mix.

Hansfor guided me to a room where all the girls were present. They were of an ecumenical make up, ranging from all skin colours, shapes, and sizes, with sexiness wrapped in common with them. I didn't think he'd give me a set of the unattractive to get me going. *But where would I go with them? I had Cindy and I certainly wouldn't give her up, no!*

'They are yours to be with you, or choose from.' The Emperor left me at this point, calling out to me, 'Enjoy.'

The door was closed and a faint giggle permeated into the chamber. I didn't know who did it, but it sounded deep and bellowed. I didn't think a Draconian Emperor would resort to that. I guessed he had something in store for me, and these women were going to give it to me. I missed Cindy already, and personally disliked my present, though inviting, situation. I was surrounded by voluptuous types you'd see on a news-stand, all coming alive at you. *Ewh!* As I had no way of communicating with her, to see how she got on, I had to pray this spellbound inconvenience would play out well.

'Oooh, so you're Silas Huer,' one of the women cooed in my ear, with her tongue, 'Come play with us.'

I wasn't in the mood for this, but as long as the concubines were full and the toddy's steaming hot, I believed I could get used to this. It was an odd addition to being Silage, though and I still thought about Cindy. It was lucky that there were no telepaths here. Draconians seemed to too practical and upfront to make way for trickery of the mind. I wouldn't put it past Silage, though, but this folk that enveloped my character were of one mind, and one purpose.

CHAPTER XII

Cindihan went on a transport to the starfield where all ships were being refurbished. She checked the original place we docked, and the *Crab* wasn't there. Looking into it, she was led to this starfield of multitudes of ships, with the possibility with ours being amongst them. She looked everywhere for our ship, thinking about me, and wishing I was here to support her. I knew with all those years grunting a life out in Anarchia, she should have some clearance in her mind for such a task.

All the ships looked the same, with imperialistic, Draconian markings on them. They weren't kidding about the Emperor's flotilla. There was a gigantic flagship in the middle of the loading bay, surrounded by smaller ships. They too had the decals on them, with all the trimmings. This grand ship definitely belonged to the Emperor.

She looked further, and soon she came across a ship that resembled *The Ancient Crab*. The markings and the paint had been changed to suit Draconian needs. The bodywork was the same, and when she looked inside, the innards of the ship displayed a darkness that lacked life all around. It looked like a ghost ship from long ago.

'This must be the *Crab*,' she thought silently.

Cindihan opened the hatch and climbed inside the ship. She tried a few switches to see what would work, if anything. *Nothing*. Meg must be thinking the enemy was tampering with the ship. This was no enemy, but how would a computer simulated voice coder know *that*? She fiddled and pressed a few more knobs when suddenly, the hatch was reopened to reveal a darker presence aboard. Well, it wasn't darker, it was just Antssarah Kane, looking over the ship for inspection. It had a scheduled flight to go on soon.

He announced, 'And what have we here?'

'Nobody special, sir,' Cindy answered.

'Nobody special, huh?' Antssarah repeated, 'You're Huer's wife, aren't you?'

She said nothing. He tried to coerce her by giving her a good smack on the face.

'Yes, yes,' she cried, 'I'm Elias's wife.'

'Ah, that's better,' he leaned closer to her, 'And are you willing to tell me what you are doing here in a secure military zone?'

'You're here,' she pouted. *Oh, those pouts of hers!*

'Yes, but I am supposed to be here. You, young lady, are not.'

'But this is the ship I came here on,' Cindy stated, throwing all caution to the wind.

'No, my dear, these are our markings. See?'

'You could have changed it to suit your wicked designs,' she spat.

'There is more to a ship than mere designs.'

Antssarah began interrogating her. This was not at all like Anarchia. There she had control. Here, she was like a baby. There was no control over her and Antssarah wasn't making it easy, either.

'What are you doing here?'

She fell silent, not wishing to reveal any secrets important to us, possibly to the Directorate. Her Anarchian instincts paid off, but Antssarah had enough with her silence.

'Guard,' he ordered, 'Take her to Hansfor. He'll know what to do with her.'

Cindihan was led away by the guard and put in a vehicle destined for the Emperor's Palace. Antssarah closed up the ship after she'd left, and drew closer to the framework. *The Ancient Crab* was still emblazoned boldly on a side she hadn't looked upon yet (before climbing in). Antssarah took a nearby blade, and removed the name, further disgracing the ship. He then grey-washed the space, shunning all responsibility and origin of our former ship, rendering it unrecognisable.

* * * * *

The girls I was with never let me down, as they cast off their silken gowns to reveal beauty beyond anyone's wildest dreams. They took me to a room with a pool in it, with a dais that resembled a lifeguard station, a few feet high.

One of the girls said to me, 'You go on that station, and choose whomever reaches you first.'

I looked up and it was mortally high to me. As Silage, I had to go through with it. Some of the girls gaily took off my clothing, barring indecency, to show off something that was really an eyeful. A lean body with a hairy chest was nothing to sniff at.

'Wow, what a body,' some of them squealed; others fainted.

'God, I want him, I want him,' another one signalled.

I started to enjoy the attention, though it was unwarranted. I was pleased that so far, I was in the game still, and, unless Cindy fails, we could both be out of here soon. This hubbub of delight was no matter, but where Cindy was concerned, I felt a pang of guilt. I was still a married man, proud of it, with a silly whiz-kid like entity for a wife. We could both high-tail it out of here, when she finds the ship and switches the console on. Meg then would fly the ship back home.

The ladies cooed and clawed their way up the rope ladder that swayed and wriggled; writhing letters with motion. Emotion was probably part of it too. As the stronger women succeeded in getting on top, there was some who didn't and fell into the water below the small dais. I remembered a distant Daye ancestor who went through such a frivolity; with people fighting, and plunging their way to the top. It was a way to elect a leader of the tribe they were in, and proved rather effective. Here, I was to pick the choicest wives, and had a little fun while doing so, though they were meant for Silage.

'Hi Silas,' one girl made it past many competitors.

'Hi,' I waved to her, 'Let me take a look at you.'

I checked her out, and she looked decent. *Not like my Cindy, though.* Even if I had Silage's mind, I still would never be Silage. I accepted her anyway, and gave her a thumbs-up before prodding her off the other side, back into the water.

This went on and on, with women bitching along, clamouring to me for affirmation. Oddly enough, all the girls who went through were allowed into the harem that was to be his. I already had a girl of my own; I could see her now, flying the *Crab*, with Meg dishing out the controls, beeping away, finding the coordinates of home. I sighed heavily.

Another lady made it up my podium, and heard the sigh I'd made. 'Oh, sorry, am I boring to you?'

'No, no,' I dismissed, 'Just...'

She peered closer. 'Just what.'

Now I had to act, *or else.* 'Just what I'd been looking for.'

I fingered her around, bits and all, showing keen interest. She smiled, and I nodded back, and flipped her over the side. She plummeted into the water, then bobbed up and waved at me. I gave her a wave and smiled pleasingly.

Gosh, I didn't know how much I could keep this up. Female after female came to me for approval, making eyes, heads and tails at me. I continued to accept them, for they were all very nice and palatable. They were most gracious to me for being part of the coolest spot on Dracos. Yet, I still worried about Cindy, and even Silage, for as he slept, I was 'taking' his women. It didn't bother me though, knowing Cindy had her task to do, and Silage was out of the ring for now. I had to hold everything up here, and this experience certainly proved a handful.

CHAPTER XIII

Silage looked good in his heady mirror, when he finally awoke from his mythological sleep. Oddly enough, he didn't remember a thing, except something he had to tell Emperor Hansfor; information which may prove useful to him, catering to Draconian interests. Technically, Silage was still *me*, but in the mirror, he only saw himself. He went through his closet to get dressed properly, something minimalistic will do. When he noticed his precious outfits had been rifled through, he, as Silage, got angry. The initial 'what the...' gave way to 'that damn, cursed brother of mine!' A favourite outfit had been taken, which made him so special; a short cut-up sleeved, open chested leather top, with matching bottoms. It was very obvious to him who would have worn such a thing, parading himself as Silage. It was yours truly, who picked the outfit to convince people that I was Silage. Of course, it took brains to be Silage, but if you had the look, you were halfway there.

He picked one of his not-so-very-charitable outfits instead, when suddenly, his insides churned intolerably, and he developed a headache, bordering on a migraine with no invasion intended. He wasn't sure if it was the spell, or just a tummy upset, but we all knew what it was. *The spell started to wear off.* He scrambled to get his clothing together, as well as himself. He then set his sights upon a nearby communicator, where he got in touch with his buddy, Silver Kane.

Kane's image appeared on the screen. 'Hello, Silas, what can I do for you? It hadn't been long since we spoke.'

A realisation went through Silage's mind. *It wasn't me, it was Elias who spoke to you Kane!*

'My darn brother is masquerading as me. I, I...'

'Silas,' Kane shouted aloud, the unit falling out of Silage's hands as he collapsed.

The spell *was* wearing off. Was it a mispronunciation or miscalculation? It was as if he had left his hair on the moon. Yet, he didn't care and prayed he would not forget the vital details of our journey. He got up and scampered out of his apartment to go to the Palace, so he may inform the Emperor that there was another universe to conquer, via the 'stargate'.

Silage swung low-key among the transports he took to get to the Emperor. His head now throbbed with magical intent, and the transformation back into himself fully. It was just the beginning for him. Though his mindset may have switched over to my own, he consciously tried to remember all the travels I'd been on. Sifting like flour to bake a cool cake, my experiences were slipping through the memory of time. He was desperately intending on fixating on that stargate and Cindihan's crazy pass-the-time doodling, which led to it.

The Palace loomed in the dark Draconian night. From his transport, Silage can see a fixed destiny. He just didn't know where it would take him. There were many lights flickering about and the cityscape looked fantastic between the mountains of Dracos. Dim and distant for now, he got off the transport and literally ran to the Palace. Was it to get to the Emperor and blab everything, or was it to get back his favourite nutty threads that I was wearing?

The guard on duty, Buckwolf, spotted him. 'Hey, didn't I see you earlier?'

Confused for a moment, Silage answered, 'No, you didn't. It was my brother, Elias you saw.'

'I'll ring the alarm.'

'No need,' Silage put his hand on the guardsman. 'Just let me through. I'll handle this. Better to take him unawares, yes?'

Buckwolf understood. 'Ummm. Good thinking. I guess that is why we've adopted you somewhat.'

Both smiled at one another, as Silage was let through. The Palace still had its deadly chic about the premises. Primed and ready, he went on a brutal hunt to find me. *The Emperor can wait.* He had a score to settle with me, first. His mind was unexpectedly in tatters, as the spell was continuing its process of dying out. The need to re-member was first and foremost in his mind, one in particular being the 'stargate'. That was his ticket out of this mess, or so he thought.

I remained with the voluptuous beauties swimming around me, swirl-ing their charms toward impossible matrimony. I would never give Cindy up for this lot. They were good, for someone. *Just not me.* I didn't care to think on them. To keep up the charade, I stood up on the dais I sat at, and dove right in. The coolness of the water was ex-hilarating, as I joined them. It put me at ease, as did the endless all-body massaging that I found myself getting from them.

Until...

I found myself in a state of disorientation. I thought it was the mas-saging, and the feel-good factor of being with all these women, Cindy notwithstanding. Now my head was starting to pound, and the personality of 'who am I?' became clear. My confidence and bravado I had shown earlier was slowly dwindling, which was scary indeed.

I didn't wish to see these women hurt by someone, who stood up to his brother in the race to get to them first. I was soon thinking of a way out of here, but if I did get out, it'd be a buckin' miracle.

* * * * *

Cindy, meanwhile was being held prisoner in one of the cells guarded by the Emperor's Special Unit. Fear had already drained her quick mind, and she hardly touched her food they gave her. This was unusual, as she was a 'pig' of sorts, loving anything that she was given, or that which she made herself. Like the unwanted soulless people of Anarchia, she felt helpless outside her already small box. She missed me and the comforts of New Chicago. The possibilities that opened up for her there were endless. She could serve the Directorate, as I was doing and make something of her life with me. It was getting later and later into the night, and sleep was the last thing on her mind. At least her mind was secure in itself, and not tampered by whiz-bang, archaic history prizes and spells of an uncertain nature.

Silage reached the prison cells before anyone else. Somehow, his choice led him there. He didn't know why, but he thought I would be confined. It made sense to him. Yet, with the last memory out of his system, he became more like himself. He soon tricked the guard with one of his clever spells, and searched for me.

And he found Cindy instead.

'Elias? Is that you, baby,' she squealed.

Not wanting to deceive any further, he came clean. 'No, it's Silas. Or Silage.'

'That's Eli's thing. I'll call you Silas,' Cindy said.

'Thank you,' he added, as he got her out of the cell and ran into another corridor.

'Before we see the Emperor, you've got to tell me what you saw before you landed on Dracos,' he pleaded, knowing now his life was at stake.

She fell silent. Then said, 'If you've got Elias's mind, you ought to know that.'

'The spell wore off, my dear,' he begged now, which was rich enough for me to want to witness. 'Come on, please. We haven't the time to argue about it.'

She still refused to answer. She liked seeing him in stitches; as a wife, she took my side. *If only I was there, too.*

'Those memories he had that I once knew are gone now. Please, love, you must tell me.'

'I am not your love,' she defied him.

The harsh boldness returned. 'We'll see about that.'

Silage took Cindy and made a quick search for me. It wasn't difficult with ladies laughter and merriment emerging from the passage. He remembered it well, as he once did this too. He enjoyed being with the ladies and what they had to offer him. The problem being was now they were offering it to *me* instead, and he did not like that one bit.

'I wonder,' Silage said aloud, a small ring of familiarity went through his mind, when he opened the door.

He dragged Cindy's pretty behind into the lounge room and into the pool area where I splashed about with the maidens of the day. The jealousy Silage felt in this situation was dead obvious. Nothing and no one could stop it. I just wanted to play a role. He wanted… well, whatever it was that he did. I could tell it wouldn't be good, though.

I got sarcastic with him; tasting my last stand of bravado. 'And you are?'

'Cut it out, Brother Elias,' Silage taunted, 'I've got your lovely wife here. She can tell us where you've been.'

'No,' I cried, fearing for Cindy. 'I already told you everything.'

'Yes, but now we tell the Emperor,' he said.

A woman popped out of the water. 'Isn't she a bit young to be a bride?'

'Yeah, her demeanour is uncannily babyish,' said another.

'Hold on, hold on, ladies,' I tried to calm myself, 'This *is* my wife. She's of age; I am not interested in babies.'

'Well, you've got one here,' one more chimed in.

And with that comment escaped the last straw of my patience. I was surprised they took that tone with Cindy. She was no baby.

Well, okay, there were aspects that screamed an infantile existence, but she was still my wife. I went to drown that woman who accused her of being a minor when Silage stuck his hand toward me, 'Elias, get out and come with me.'

I paused, I hesitated, then I went away from the girls. I jumped out of the water with regret to follow Silage. I was given a towel to dry off with and dressed quickly in a robe.

'You're very lucky, Brother Elias,' he warned me, 'You had better co-operate with Hansfor or we'll all be in for it.'

'Don't worry, Silage,' I answered, 'I promise to behave.'

'The star…,' he choked on the word 'stargate', for some reason.

Cindy showed concern for Silage. 'You okay?'

'Yes, sweetness, I am.'   He turned to her. 'I just wish you would tell us about the star….'

He fell back again. I stood him up, and tried to revive him. He came to, and thanked me. It was lucky that Silage hadn't put a gun on me, nor Cindy. Maybe there was a better way out of this.

CHAPTER XIV

Silage took me in to meet with the Emperor Hansfor. Not that I hadn't met him before, as *Silage*. I felt embarrassed at this forthcoming insult, that my true identity as Elias will be revealed to him. The Emperor basked on his throne, with a girl filing his nails. He looked a real treat to them, if they were into that sort of thing. He had a son, who was just as attractive, and youthful, which gave the ladies an advantage to pursue him, instead of the father.

The sharp-shooter mindset though, was thinning faster than an old man's scalp, as I approached the throne area. I gulped, and the sweat tingled in the hairs of my chest. Silage looked smarter than me, oddly enough, especially when he felt he had the advantage. Yet I, in a quasi-disciplined way, felt more in control, or tried to. Cindy didn't know what to make of it and simply fainted. Women, once skirting the walls to bask in the sunlight, leapt toward her to see if she was alright. Silly thing was, they were medics as well, so if anything really were to happen, they could help her.

'Hold on, hold on,' the Emperor shouted, 'What's the meaning of this?'

Carefully, he peered at Silage and I. He shook his head, as if he was seeing double which he was. I didn't speak, so Silage did so, instead.

'Your Excellency,' he began boldly, 'I know the secret behind my brother's journey here.'

My heart sank, and I prayed to whatever God was listening.

'Yes,' Hansfor nodded, bidding his time, 'I'm with you.'

Silage cleared his throat. 'My Lord, my brother Elias and his wife Cindy had discovered a star...'

He choked again, and just to be on the safe side, I punched Silage in the mouth, which caused a bleeding lip. The guards held me to, and Cindy just awoken.

She cried, 'Elias?'

'Shh,' I whispered to her, 'Not now.'

'You, Elias?' The Emperor got up to look me over. 'You are very cunning. You thought I would believe you to be Silas, right? And why would that have been? What is this star thing you discovered?'

Cindy yelled, 'Elias!'

Silage came to, and touched his bleeding lip. He wanted revenge for this, but not here. Things were hotting up as it is.

He tried again, anyway, for good measure. 'They discovered a star...'

He bowled over again, this time for real. Not due to anyone physically touching him violently, except that the spell he put himself under now rendered him incapable of revealing the little secret of that stargate, the most vital aspect of this visit. *It was nothing I did.* That was why I disliked magic in the first place. Spells and trickery were part of deception. I hated deception. It all comes back to you anyway, so what was the point of it all?

All his thoughts about the stargate, and whatever else he had stored in his brain were drained out of him, and he became Silage, alone.

No further impact regarding myself was in his mind anymore. It was just him and his memories, *alone*.

Hansfor had enough of this, and looked at me. 'You, you Elias can help us. You may wear your brother's clothing, but I know the difference. What did you and your wife discover before you came here?'

I looked down at myself to see I only wore that robe for modesty. It was an embarrassment for me, being seen like this, instead of my formal neck-collar suits I was accustomed to wearing in New Chicago. The feelings of home sank in my imagination, if there was one, and I began to wish I hadn't come along on this wild ride, just to discover a mere *stargate*. What was worse, I had been swinging with those girls and had a good time, before Silage ruined it for me. I felt I made a right shamble out of everything. Not that it was *my* fault, you see.

I gave the same lame banter I gave everyone else. 'It's actually just a bunch of asteroids and a dead star, nothing more.'

'No, no, there is more,' the Emperor panted at me. 'I know you found something, and it would help you to help us, or I kill your wife.'

Suddenly, one of the Emperor's guards took Cindy and pulled a gun on her. She nearly screamed, when both Silage and I yelled, 'NO!'

Hansfor insisted, 'Then tell us what you'd been up to! I don't really see what the big deal is about anyway. Is it a big deal?'

'It's just that star and asteroids, sir,' I whimpered, 'You can make a great game of them.'

'And I can make a great game of YOU.' He was about to force cuffs on me, when Silage fell over in a heap, with a cloudy, gassy head.

The guard spoke gruffly, 'What's with him?'

The Emperor looked at me with concern, 'Well?'

I had to tell him; but I faked it. 'Look, I only wanted to see a larger scope outside of Earth, with a short visit with my brother. Silage put both of us under a spell, and...'

A scream was emitted from Silage, as the after effects of the spell smashed him down, and gave him a splitting headache.

To which he asked, 'Anyone got an aspirin?'

The Emperor motioned to one of the ladies to get him something for relief. He then said, 'Remove them for detention. I'll deal with this later.'

'But,' Silage started to say.

Hansfor said, 'I've got no patience for the likes of either of you, but I am willing to give you a second chance. Don't blow it.'

The guards led us out to the prison block, which was dark, dim and not a place you would take your date to. We were kept away from the other prisoners, due to the importance we were to the Emperor. I knew that if the Draconians knew about the stargate, havoc would wreak in this galaxy, as well as others. I didn't want that, and I trust my fellow Earth comrades wouldn't want this either.

It seemed scary to think the people of Dracos would want more. Why would that be possible? Dracos as an average sized moon seemed ideal. Not too large, not too small. I could not imagine what would happen if they knew about the stargate, and what worlds they could spread themselves into. *By settlement, or by conquest?*

By looking at the aggressive, dominating nature of the Emperor, and his people, the cultural influences, and the self-discipline, I would bank on conquest. No, I mulled through this before. *That's what I would do, if I wanted to get anywhere in life.* These people would be no exception.

The cell looked dingy, a far cry from the pleasurable pools and women from the other side of the Palace. I wonder if they missed me yet. I missed them, somewhat. They were lovely and kind to me, but I sensed they knew and tasted aggression.

'I cannot believe you didn't tell his Excellency about the...,' Silage started to choke again on the final word.

I asked, 'Pardon?'

'Sounds like someone's holding the tongue,' Cindy observed.

'Yeah,' I continued, 'It's that spell he put on us, to change our personalities. He used it to get to this information, and oh, how it backfired.'

I chuckled at his expense, knowing I had the major advantage. We sat in the cell, thinking of what to say, without giving up knowledge of the stargate. It will be some time before the Emperor would see us again, possibly for a final time.

CHAPTER XV

A clock on the wall read 3.23 pm. A guard at the door scowled at us, like a television star of old who relished in being a tough fellow. He gave us our lunch, begrudgingly, passing it through like a letterbox. It was meagre Draconian fare; nothing but a bit of bread and a slap of meat to get your insides going. I ate both, while Silage eyeballed Cindy. Now he remembered himself, and began to make passes at her. Too bad I was on full throttle at the time.

And this time was no different. 'No, Silage, please, not her,' I began to threaten him, 'You may know where we've been, but you ain't takin' my wife.'

'I know not to take your wife, but she is most flattering, isn't she?' He smiled at me, 'I do know where you've been Elias. I had your thoughts and memories, as you may recall.'

'I had yours,' I snapped back. 'So what of it?'

'I know you found a star...'

He choked again. *What was it about that word 'stargate'?* Ah, I remembered now. It was in the spell.

Cindy ran to him, unconquered, and obviously unbiased. 'Silas, are you okay?'

'Yes, Cindy, thank you.' He appreciated her sentiment towards him.

She gave him some of her food, and I let her play nursemaid for a bit. Maybe his influence could get us off this rock of a planet. It was a daring hope, but a hope nonetheless.

I watched them, and called out to her, 'Take care of him, but remember who you are.'

'I know,' she called back at me. 'Cindihan Huer. Got it.'

'Good, or you will get it.'

She went to me, forgiving the play-bravado I was putting on her. 'Look Elias, you needn't be jealous. I love you more than anything, and when we leave here, I will prove to you a most generous wife.'

She showed me her middle.

'You're, you're...'

I fainted. It explained why Cindy didn't want to pursue the stargate and beyond. It also explained her recent jittery behaviour.

'Elias,' Silage cried, coming to me.

'At least, I know it's his,' she explained to him.

What a way to spend time in confined detention. When I came to, we were surrounded by guards, Buckwolf was among them.

'Last trip to the throne room for you all,' he sneered at us, 'Then, who knows?'

We were led back to the royal chambers, not knowing if we were to live or die. I still refused to reveal the stargate, or its location to the Draconians. *Let them find it themselves.*

Soon, we were in the presence of Emperor Hansfor. He seemed placid, deceptively so, petting the water animals that edged the throne itself. They resembled a mix of crocodile, alligator, and a whole load of yuck. They were effective for a quick bite, and prisoners were their tasty favourites.

Hansfor said, 'So, have you decided to tell us about your discovery, or will my pets eat it out of you?'

Maybe it was time to discuss that stargate after all.

Suddenly, before I was able to speak, a courier ran through the room, unhindered by guards. This was a personal dispatcher who served the Emperor and his, alone.

'Your Majesty, I apologise for the intrusion,' he puffed, 'But this message came directly for you. I think it will be of interest.'

The Emperor stared at the courier with eyes like his water pets, and took the note from him. After he waved the courier off, he quietly read the communique. It brought unexpected news. Thankfully, good news.

'My son, my son. I have... I have,' he spluttered insanely, nearly fainting.

I saw a person very familiar to Silage and me. It was Antssarah Kane, the one we used to call Antsy. *God, what was he doing here?* I knew he served Dracos like his brother Silver, but to be *this* close to the Emperor?

Antssarah looked over his shoulder. 'What, your Excellency?'

It was odd to see him after all these years. Those park days were so long ago. I'd forgotten how good they were. Such friendships being tossed to the wind over a stupid doodle that led to the stargate were flimsy at best, but I never thought of my friendship with him as that. I really liked him back then, and wished to recapture those experiences. It felt like he went over to the 'other' side now, and nothing of our friendship could return again.

The Emperor went over to Antssarah Kane, and gave him a hug and kiss, a very odd thing for a Draconian Emperor to do. This better be good.

'I'm a grandfather,' he declared. 'My son Draco has a daughter!'

'Congratulations, Your Excellency,' Antssarah bowed to him. 'Now what about these prisoners?'

Still in a euphoric state, Hansfor, merely dismissed us. Wishing to ignore everything to the wind, he knew we weren't going to tell him what we saw. He was too giddy to give orders to finish us off, either. The newly-born child meant the world to him. *His world.* His lineage could continue. It was a good thing to breed about in the mind, so he gave us an ultimatum.

'I will grant leniency to you Silas, Elias, and Cindihan Huer. You have failed to give me the information I requested, preventing vital progress within my society. This makes you utterly useless and we are a burgeoning Empire. I intend to keep it this way. We will grow and we will conquer the universe as we see fit, whether or not you tell us where you've been. We are just as good as you and maybe we will discover what you found. No matter, a grandchild is more important, and you lot are finished here.

'My son Draco had his first born daughter, Ardala, delivered today. Maybe they will see through your works of treachery; maybe Ardala herself will come to rule and find out your discovery. Whatever it is, will wait. Your ship is to be ready for you at the space dock and you have to leave immediately, never to return here again. Count yourself lucky; if it weren't for Ardala, I'd have the three of you here permanently, alive or dead. Now go!'

He turned his back on us and went into an antechamber, leading to another part of the Palace where that little girl was born. It would be a wonder how that little girl turned out to be.

Antssarah and a few guardsmen, including Buckwolf, led us away to take us to the ship, and turned to us. 'So your turnabouts were quite fruitful, then?'

Cindy didn't speak to him, as a laser-gun bolt was aimed at her once more. Silage and I kept quiet as well.

'That's what we think of traitors,' Buckwolf threatened.

I argued back, 'How could we be traitors if we didn't tell you anything, or do anything to hurt you?'

'You didn't tell us what we wanted. Silas here fled to our cause, and yet said nothing to us regarding your discovery.'

'I would have,' Silage begged.

'I know you would, but no, you kept silent like your brother here,' Antssarah carried on.

He took the gun from Buckwolf and fired it on poor Cindy. She fell
down, gasping for breath.

'Cindy,' I cried.

'She's dead, Elias,' Antssarah taunted me, 'But we will find out what
you know. Meanwhile, you have nothing.'

He laughed wickedly, as I carried her as we made our way to the
Crab, despite its newly-done Draconian markings upon it. I knew it
was our ship, and Meg was somewhere hiding in endless consoles
within it. We boarded, and Silage laid Cindy on a makeshift bed. It
was hard, but she had to be flat out; we needed to tend to her wound.

Buckwolf joined us, and oddly enough helped us with Cindy. It felt
like a wasted, hasty journey coming here. Yet, deep down, I felt a
surge of something else. Nothing like what I experienced during the
switching 'spell' with Silage. Nothing like getting your wife killed
for no reason, and for something that was out there, waiting to be discovered. *So why couldn't they? Why take the girl of my dreams!??*

Soon, we were in orbit, and I still hadn't activated Meg. I remained
on manual control, due to the sensitivity of Meg. I dared not reveal
anything else Earth had available to this Draconian. Silage was
caring for Cindy, trying to mend her.

'She won't live much longer,' Buckwolf guffawed.

Silage's eyes became the wild young boy I recalled seeing as a child;
the wonder of discovery, and the wonder of magic.

To which he screamed out a short chant, and Buckwolf was himself spellbound. I put the control on auto-pilot, while I left my seat to search for a gun. I found one and used it on Buckwolf, but I only stunned him. *Put him back to dozy-land*, I figured.

'Well, that's rid of him,' I sighed, 'Silage, find a compartment, or air-lock and get him in it. Then take care of Cindy.'

'I'll find a compartment. An airlock would be too risky. You know that, Elias,' Silage answered.

Ha-ha, I smirked, and I threw the switch on Meg.

'Oh, wow, whew, that was a long sleep,' she awoken. 'Elias?'

'Yeah, it's me. You take over. There are more pressing matters,' I added, and left the seat.

'Whatever you say. It's nice to see you again.'

That was a weird thing coming from a computer. The controls started moving by themselves, as we were on a new heading toward Earth. I stayed with Cindy, as I cradled her in my arms. She was barely breathing, and I prayed she'd last so a medic could look at her.

'You both are rather quiet today,' Meg noticed.

'Cindy's been shot, and we're looking after her,' I replied.

'Looks like we'd have to grab a speedy return, then,' she propelled the ship on its course.

'I do hope she makes it,' Silage confessed to me.

I shot back, 'Why, so you could have my wife?'

'Please Elias, not now. We have to care for her,' he cuddled her lov-
ingly.

'I'll do that, thank you,' I intoned aggressively at him. I sat beside
her, switching seats with Silage.

A small voice uttered, 'You'll always be with me, Elias?'

'Yes, Cindy, I'll always be with you. I love you, dear.'

I hugged her, as I felt the life inside draining away. *Come on, come
on, a few quadrants more.* Meg did the best she could on a tight
schedule. Well, it was not really a schedule, as we had no real ties to
be anywhere, except where we belonged: Earth. I begged God to
save my love. I didn't know what to do, and I thought it would be the
end of us, for now.

CHAPTER XVI

Suddenly, a ship with similar markings and make of *The Ancient Crab* shot into view. Meg flashed it on screen, as Silage took over the monitor. It was a friendly ship, one of ours. In fact, it was the *Noble Gray*.

Silage rang out desperately into the comm unit. 'This is *The Ancient Crab*. If you can hear us, please come in.'

Fortunately, a voice came over. 'This is Lt Selina Cayley of the Earth Defence Directorate. May I be of assistance?'

Thank God, we were nearing Earth, at last!

'This is Silas Huer. Elias and his wife are aboard. There is also a Draconian aboard as well, but he'd been detained in a storage unit. I will need medical help immediately. The wife's been shot.'

'Acknowledged. I will get a medical team together. Ready your flight, and follow on my mark, one-lemur-pantha-serina. Over.'

'Got it. Thanks,' Silage signed off.

Meg had the controls which led the ship to Earth. I couldn't hold out any longer, and it would have been nice to let the Directorate know that I was okay. *Silly Silage!*

'I wanted to say hello, you know,' I said.

'Cindy's more important right now.' He turned to me, 'You continue to look after her. Besides, we're almost there.'

Silage pointed out the Earth in the close-range distance.

'You like to follow on her mark no doubt,' I sneered sarcastically.

'Maybe. Mark one, steady as she goes,' he concentrated on the controls, despite Meg's auto-pilot.

I loved it how he wanted to out-do me at the controls of a ship that I had piloted before: the ship I found the stargate with! We flew toward the Earth, and the Cayley escort was present. It was like returning right back, before the madness began. Thankfully, we landed safely and Cindy was quickly whisked away and wheeled to sickbay, with Dr Wildock leading the team that *may* save her. It was Lt Cayley's actions that allowed my dearest to get that fair chance at life she so deserved, now that she was in a safe place.

Despite this, I felt terrible that I had a potential casualty on my hands, when Pemur and Cayley approached me and Silage.

Pemur was most adamant. 'What the buck happened out there? Elias, you should know better.'

I looked at him, and then at my dopey brother, who got us all into this mess, then looked afar to Cindy who was just turning the corner, and I broke down and cried bitterly.

Silage took over and explained, 'He lost his wife.'

'No, damn you Silage,' I yelled, 'There may be a chance to save her.'

'Alright, alright already,' Silage backed down, quite easily in fact. I was not used to this.

'Yes,' Pemur nodded, 'I've heard. I am sorry, but we have to let the doctors do their work. It may take time.'

'I want her back now,' I ranted, 'Not cold honest fact!'

Silage saw the folly of his magical journey and offered to help me.

'The stun they used on her was close to deadly. Draconians use that to topple their enemies,' he glumly remarked.

'That Draconian you stashed aboard your ship is being detained and will be returned to the Saturn moon,' Cayley said.

Pemur looked at Silage with suspicion. 'You did not tell the Draconians about the discovery, did you?'

Silage relented, sighed and further explained, 'I would have, if it weren't for my clever brother here. The spell I made to find out about this had worn off and...'

'What spell?' Pemur threw a rampage. 'You used magic? You go into someone else's territory, planning to inform them of something *we* did? '

I suddenly got playful, in order to 'save' Silage. 'Nothing like a little bing-bong spell to fool the Draconians, eh?'

'I don't believe this,' Pemur insisted, 'We are men of medicine, science, and...'

I interrupted him, and shouted at the top of my lungs. 'Then save my wife, for God's sake, man!'

'We're getting there,' he assured me. 'She's in good hands; we have the best doctors this side of the Rockies.'

'The Rockies don't exist anymore,' I whimpered, 'It's all Anarchia. Where did you think I found my girl in the first place???!!'

Cayley, Pemur and Silage saw me at my worst and tried to be em-pathetic about it.

'Let's go to the deck room for leisure,' Cayley suggested, 'We may be in there a long time.'

'I think she will be okay,' Pemur held my arm, and then gave me a hug. 'I've known you nearly all your life. It pains me to see you like this.'

'I'm sorry,' I whined, 'I'm so...'

I broke down, hoping he was right about Cindy. Silage lent over to me in support, and prayed his archaic prayers. I tried to listen, but it was no good. My concentration was all on Cindy. *Darn it.* I could not get her out of my mind, though I was thankful that Silage had left it. At least now my memories will remain my own. No further tam-pering needed.

Pemur and Cayley led us to the deck room, where some drinks were ordered and more tears were shed. The clock ticked the vital minutes that led to final hours. I detested being there, and preferred to be alone for the moment. I knew the doctors would be helpful, but even in the 25th century, people die. Everybody goes, no matter where or *when* you live.

I refused to believe my dear Cindy would go in the direction of the dead. *She couldn't.* I never ever thought of religion as a comfort, even the plain-jane style we use today. My mind raced toward some form of rest, and I began to mentally be still. I now prayed, hoping it wouldn't be the end of us.

TO BE CONTINUED....